THE HUNDREDTH TIME AROUND

A NOVEL

STACY LEE

FRENCH MARTINI PRESS

THE HUNDREDTH TIME AROUND by Stacy Lee

Copyright © 2021 by Stacy Lee

French Martini Press

Salem, New Hampshire

Cover Art- Spark Creative

🏵 Created with Vellum

ACKNOWLEDGMENTS

First and foremost, I would like to thank Lynn and her team at Red Adept Editing. Your notes and corrections were extremely helpful, and your team was phenomenal to work with. The editing stage of the writing process has never been my favorite. Thank you for making it easy.

Also, I want to give a special thank you to Julie and the staff at Spark Creative. Thank you for bringing the ideas we discussed regarding the cover art to life. Thank you for listening to my suggestions, for being so professional, and for making it fun.

Thank you, Pam Claughton, for showing me the ropes and for guiding me through the journey of independent publishing. I can't thank you enough.

Thank you to everyone who helped with my manuscript. Thank you, Kara Holloway, Marisa Berlin, and Karen DeBruyckere, for reading through my very rough first draft and for being so supportive. A big thank you to my sister, Kate Giglio and my friend Stacie Swanson for always cheering me on.

A huge thank you to my husband, Paul Barbagallo. I love

you to the moon and back and I am forever grateful to have found a man who is so loving and encouraging. I love living my dreams with you.

Thank you to the community of York, Maine. The memories we made on Short Sands beach will always be dear to my heart. Thank you, Shirley Barbagallo, for bringing me to the Nubble Lighthouse for the first time. Your idea to sketch and paint the beautiful landmark very well may be the reason this story came about. We love you and will keep you forever in our hearts.

I would like to thank my children, Paul and Lucy. Follow your dreams and listen to your hearts. Stay true to who you are and don't be afraid to give second chances. Nobody is perfect, and we don't always get it right the first time. Follow your heart, honor God, and be nice to your mother. (You can read my book when you are eighteen).

I also need to thank my friend Jessica Delano. Thank you for sitting on the beach with me on that fourth of July and for inspiring me with the story of your relative who rented beach property years ago. My fictional world has never been the same.

I am grateful for my parents, Karen and Daniel DeBruyckere, for teaching me, "If I can think it, I can do it." Thank you for always believing in me.

Last but not least, I need to thank you, the reader! Thank you for picking up this book. You aren't just holding a story in your hands; you are holding my dream come true. I hope you fall in love with the characters like I have. May you be inspired to stick your toes in the ocean and spend your days searching for sea glass, clam shells, and dreams with those you love.

FOR SHIRLEY J. BARBAGALLO

(1953-2020)
"All your dreams are real."

PROLOGUE

The intensity of his gaze as he stared down at the sand between his bare toes would make a person stop and wonder if he was counting the grains. He wasn't counting anything, actually, other than his uninvited tears. He didn't want to cry in front of her. He didn't cry in front of anybody.

She reached out and grasped his hand. The calluses on his fingertips brushed ever so slightly against hers, so slightly that they almost didn't touch. But she knew they were there. She had practically memorized every detail about him: how he awkwardly brushed one hand through the hair on the back of his head when he was nervous, the steady rhythm of his heartbeat when he held her in his arms, the way he smelled first thing in the morning, the look of melancholy in his eyes when she pleaded that he stay.

Except today. Today, there was no begging. No asking. There was just silence. How could there be words on a day like this? There would be no laughing, no dancing, no dreaming of tomorrow. On a day like today, there was only room for goodbye.

PART ONE

SUMMER OF 2001

SUMMER OF 2001 CASSIDY

CHAPTER ONE

*T*he frigidity of the ocean water startled me as it slapped up against my ankles. I should have known better than to comb the beach during high tide. Had Grandma taught me nothing? I would never find anything good out here tonight. My thoughts skipped and scattered, kind of like how my Pearl Jam CD was skipping in my head-phones. Why was it that when I made an effort to clear my head, it felt most cluttered? I tossed away the broken clam shell I had just pulled out of the soggy muck and wiped my hands on my shorts. I clutched my Discman horizontally in front of me in an effort to stop the skipping. *It's just you and me, Eddie Vedder. You, me, and the sea.*

It had been days since Emma and I had moved into our summer beach rental. My twenty-second birthday had been spent lugging boxes and suitcases into our tiny version of paradise. The Seaberry felt like more of a cabin than a beach house, really. The rustic maple woodwork that framed the walls and ceilings was welcoming. I sensed immediately the familiar vibe that this house had once been loved. For some, it might have seemed too small or too many miles from shore. But to two twentysomething girls straight out of undergrad, it signified nothing but a summer of possibility.

I lost my train of thought once again due to the breathtaking view before me. I stared out at the horizon and the open water. The ocean went on farther than I could imagine. Long, thin but puffy cumulus clouds stacked against each other in rows with tiny spaces in between, allowing the smallest bit of light to peek through. Aside from a few sailboats in the distance, the water was all I could see. The surfers and tourists were gone for the evening. Pearl Jam wasn't skipping anymore. Eddie's voice was raspy and intoxicating, and I breathed in the salt from the air.

I inhaled again, and the dampness of salt mixed with wind took my breath away. Sometimes it seemed almost impossibly easy for the sea to calm my anxieties.

"Hey!"

As a hand on my shoulder jolted me back to reality, I stopped in my tracks and jumped at least two feet off the ground. I gasped, unable to catch my breath, as my heart raced and thudded. I lost my footing as I tried to get a look at this person who had invaded my calm beach moment. I tripped over an unexpected rock, almost dropping my Discman. I didn't know this guy. But the hand, his hand, reached down and caught my device centimeters before it hit the water.

"I'm sorry! Can I help you?" I exploded. I stood up as fast as I could, brushing wet sand off my denim cutoffs.

"Calm down, there, killer!" He laughed.

"Calm down? You can't just frolic around the beach, grabbing girls! You're lucky I didn't kick you in the…"

He looked amused. He stared at me for a beat. "Kick me in the what?"

I rolled my eyes, but he smiled back and handed me my Discman. I nodded my thanks and plugged my headphones back into the jack, trying with great effort to get my hands to stop shaking.

"What are you listening to?"

I chuckled as if to say "No way, not gonna happen" and turned to face the other direction, very much aware that we were the only two people on Long Sands Beach.

"Are you just going to walk away?"

I turned, paused, and checked him over. He didn't appear to be a serial killer or a stalker, but what did those really look like? I wished I had a cell phone like Emma did. I would flip it open and call 911. But instead, I speedily studied his profile just in case I needed to give the police a description later on. I imagined myself sitting at the station like they did on TV, trying to give an estimate of his height, when all I could really tell at this moment was that he was taller than me (six foot one maybe?) with brown hair and dark eyes. They would want to know his weight, but I stank at that, and I was distracted by his dimples.

"I don't talk to strangers," I sassed, satisfied with my response. I continued strutting away from him and carefully placed my headphones over my ears.

He touched my shoulder again. I flicked his hand off. "Are you nuts?" It was more like a statement than a question.

He froze and held both hands in front of his face as if to say he surrendered. It wasn't until now that I realized that whoever he was, he was actually kind of cute. I sighed and turned to face him. His lips curled into a smile, and he extended his hand to mine to shake it.

"Sean," he stated. "Sean Anderson."

I was hesitant to shake his hand, but when I did, I was surprised at how mine didn't feel cold until now.

"Cassidy," I replied as if I was repeating my McDonald's order for the third time.

"Well, Cassidy." He retrieved his hand from mine and put

both of his hands in his pockets. "I was only trying to tell you that I think you have a beautiful voice."

I blushed. I hadn't realized that I had been singing out loud. I shook my head as if to say "Not going to happen" again and hung my headphones around my neck.

"Pearl Jam," I mumbled. "I was listening to Pearl Jam." I turned and continued walking. "It was nice to meet you, Sean."

I didn't turn back around even once. But as I changed course and cut through the center of the beach and up the steps to the parking lot, there was no doubt in my mind that he remained close behind.

* * *

"Did you find any?"

"You are going to have to be a little more specific." I playfully tapped Emma on her shoulder.

She rolled her eyes. "Any sea glass?"

"No. It was high tide. Not so sure if Long Sands kicks up much of that. Maybe I'll try Short Sands next time. But I did…kind of…meet someone though," I mumbled.

"How do you *kind of* meet someone?"

Emma stirred the spaghetti on the stove in the small kitchen. Hot steam surrounded the pan as she reached in with a fork and pulled out a fresh, squirmy noodle. She tossed it at me, and I caught it in midair, flinching briefly as it scalded the tips of my fingers. I blew on it and then sucked it up, making a popping sound with my lips.

"Is it done?"

"Al dente," I mumbled while chewing.

"A few more minutes then," she decided. "Anyways, don't change the subject. How do you sort of meet someone? And who was it?"

"I met a guy," I started. But I didn't get anything else out before she was in my face, her brown eyes popping out of their sockets like something from a horror movie.

"*Hello?*" she shrieked. "Um, '*by the way*, Emma, I met a guy.'"

"It wasn't like that. He wasn't anything special."

"Oh dear, Cassidy," she sang with dramatic flair. "That right there is how you know he actually is."

I stared blankly at my friend. After a few breaths and with no comeback in sight, I replied, "Hey, Em. The spaghetti is done."

"What's his name?" she asked, obviously ignoring me.

I twirled a strand of my red tresses around my finger. Playing nervously with my hair was a trait I had inherited from my mother and grandmother. All three of us shared the same hair and eye color. As a child, I had never liked being called Pippi Longstocking but was okay with Anne from *Anne of Green Gables*. Anne with an E, they would call me. Hair as red as strawberries and eyes as green as the sea.

"HELLO?"

I walked toward the fridge and brushed past Emma, who followed me around with a fork, waving it almost frantically in the air. I took the fork from her, grabbed the metal strainer, and dropped it into the tiny sink.

"You really need to get a life." I chuckled. I stepped back, and steam exploded in front of me as I drained the pasta.

"What was his name?" she repeats.

"Sean, I think."

"Where does he live? What does he look like?"

I opened a jar of sauce and added it to the pasta pan, pretending that I didn't care to talk about Sean, his residence, or his physical description, when the reality was that the thought of him consumed me.

"I don't know where he lives. I was over by the rocks at

Long Sands, and I don't really remember what he looked like," I lied again, thinking back to the description I had been ready to give the police. I was certain that I would end up mentioning the curve of his half smile and the familiarity of his brown eyes. I stirred the sauce and shrugged. I pictured his face: his defined cheekbones, his dark-brown hair, the way his biceps peeked through his white T-shirt just enough… "He had brown hair," I said.

"That's a start," she replied, using her teacher voice. "Our age?"

"Maybe," I answered. "Maybe a little older?"

We both leaned over the kitchen counter with our bowls. Emma turned to me with a mouthful of food. "I like the mystery guy." She giggled, slurping a piece of pasta into her mouth. The sauce splattered the side of her face, and she wiped it away with the back of her hand.

"I guess," I replied, trying to match her tone.

She adjusted the elastic holding her ponytail. It was so black in color that it camouflaged itself into the pile of thick, dark hair on the top of her head.

"Anyways," I started, "let's talk about work tomorrow."

"Blah," she whined. "Boring."

"It's our first day." I giggled. "Aren't you the least bit excited?"

"Excited?" She dropped her fork. "Excited to wait tables at the lighthouse?"

"Yes." I nodded. "Excited to make some cash so I can begin to chip away at the cost of four years of undergrad. And it's not a lighthouse. The restaurant is next to the lighthouse."

"Right." She nodded. "The Nimble."

"No." I laughed. "It's the Nubble Lighthouse."

"I'm excited to make money," she replied, ignoring my correction.

I smiled and nodded. A friend of her mother's had set us

up with jobs. Our plan was to spend the summer waitressing and enjoying the perks of living by the ocean. Then Emma would finish up her bachelor's degree with her student teaching, and I would continue with my education in Boston at Harvard Law. That would only be made possible by my own blood, sweat, and tears (and a few scholarships), whereas Emma would graduate in a few years with not one student loan, her master's fully paid for by her parents.

"Anyways," I continued, slurping up the last of my pasta, "we need to leave by eleven o'clock tomorrow." I placed my dish in the sink and started to rinse it out. "I was thinking that we could hit the beach in the morning?"

"And try to find Mystery Guy?" She giggled.

I tossed the sponge at my friend, and it hit her square in the face. She laughed and chucked it back at me. I caught it and continued washing our dishes, distracted by thoughts of tomorrow and what the summer could bring. The idea of seeing him again tickled my insides in a way that wasn't so familiar but was a tiny bit fantastic.

SUMMER OF 2001- CASSIDY

CHAPTER TWO

*E*mma liked to drive with the windows down. It wasn't usually my thing, but I made an exception because, well, because of a couple of things, really. There was the way the salt air felt as it kissed my face, for starters, and then also that overwhelming low-tide dead-fish smell that would turn most stomachs. That was one of my favorite smells in the whole world.

I hadn't always been this obsessed with the beach. But on evenings like this, when the sun was going down and people had vacated the shore for the day, those were the times that I felt closest to my family, especially Grandma.

Sometimes I played a game I called First Times. I shut my eyes really tight and thought really hard about the first memory I had of a place or an event. Some were foggy and some were not, like the first time I rode a bike without training wheels or my first experience swimming without a life jacket. I remembered that as if it was yesterday, the invigorating feeling of my head sinking under the water, unable to bring myself back up. When I was younger, I would approach my parents with my best guess, and they would confirm or deny, to the best of their abilities, whether my memory was accurate. Either way, they were always able to spin each experience as being nothing but wonderful.

As I sat in the passenger seat of Emma's car, I couldn't help but feel the dread in the pit of my stomach. The feeling had never quite gone away. It was a constant reminder that now, no matter how good my guesses were, I would have to simply live with the uneasiness of never knowing if I was right or wrong, because now there was nobody left to ask.

Emma, who appeared to sense my moment of melancholy, playfully nudged me on the shoulder and asked, "Beers and sea glass?"

To anyone else, this might have sounded like an odd combination, but not to us. I nodded and was suddenly eager to put the day of serving steamers and cocktails to hungry tourists behind me.

* * *

Just under an hour later, Emma and I were combing the beach for treasure, red Solo cups in hand. As I bent down to pick up an emerald-green piece of sea glass, tiny amounts of ocean water mixed in with my beer, and I laughed.

"Now that's a new invention," she snickered. "Sea salt on the rocks."

I laughed too, handing her my cup so I could stick the sea glass into the pocket of my shorts and fix the top of my ponytail.

Emma made a face, and her eyebrows rose in curiosity as she gazed behind me. "Who is that?"

"Who?" I took my cup from her hand and sipped from it, turning around.

I knew who it was before I looked. I would have been lying if I'd said that I hadn't been thinking about him for the entire walk—or for the entire day for that matter. As we approached him, sitting on the beach between clusters of rocks in a low folding chair, I took a swig of my beer and wiped my hair out of my eyes. I could tell that he wasn't on the beach alone, but it wasn't until we got closer that I could make out that the person he was sitting with was a man much older than him, elderly in a great-grandfather sort of way.

"I knew you couldn't stay away," he teased through his smile.

The return of his dimple made my knees weak. "I didn't realize you owned the beach," I sighed. "My mistake."

"I'm Emma."

He took her hand in his and accepted the handshake.

I paused for a moment and turned toward the gentleman to Sean's right. His body was turned away from us, facing the ocean as if our entire conversation did not exist. We didn't exist. Whatever movie was playing in his mind clearly had nothing to do with our childish banter. His blue United States Navy cap was pulled down over most of his face, and his mouth was hidden under the collar of his sweatshirt. Realizing that the man was not going to engage in our exchange, I turned away from him and messed with my hair.

"Hello. I'm Cassidy," I said with a smirk.

"Well, now. That wasn't too hard, was it?" he joked.

I rolled my eyes and pulled my hand back, glancing again at the other man.

"This is Grandpa," Sean explained. He gently pulled Grandpa's cap away from his face, examined him, and then looked back at us. "Grandpa is taking his daily nap, but I'm sure he would say it's nice to meet you both."

Sean set the cap back in place and playfully rubbed the older man's shoulders as if to warm him up. Grandpa didn't budge, but Sean chuckled as if they were exchanging laughs and looked back at me. As his eyes met mine, they were suddenly softer somehow.

"You guys have met?" Emma asked.

I love her, I thought. Of course, by now, she had put two and two together and deduced that this was the mystery guy I'd met yesterday. I was thankful for her discretion and nodded.

"Yesterday, right here on the beach," Sean said.

"Yeah, he tried to give me a heart attack," I accused.

"By rescuing your Discman?"

"Something like that." I ignored the heat from my cheeks and the tingle in my chest.

"Hey." He laughed. "It isn't every day I hear the voice of an angel."

My heart stopped beating, and my words were lost. Voice of an angel? I took a sip of my beer and turned toward Emma, hoping he wasn't noticing my pink face. My words became lost in the moment. "Music," I managed to mutter.

"Pearl Jam, huh?" Emma declared as if diagnosing my terminal illness.

Emma despised Pearl Jam. When I gave her a hard time about it, she insisted that it was the same thing as my hatred of yogurt. I liked the look of it and the texture of it, but I just couldn't quite appreciate the taste. I mean, she wasn't wrong. It was kind of the same thing, but who wouldn't like to taste Eddie Vedder?

"Yes, Pearl Jam."

"Well, I would have been crazy not to introduce myself," Sean affirmed.

I started to get a little annoyed at his confidence and borderline cocky attitude, but then his arm was around Grandpa's shoulders, and I was useless again. I nodded and sipped my beer.

* * *

SOME NIGHTS WERE WORSE than others. I'd gotten used to staring into the darkness at all hours of the night, wondering how things could have been different. It was another game I played with myself. I called it If Only. Some things triggered my panic attacks, and some things didn't. It was all linked to my "condition," as the doctors like to call it. My therapist had bigger words for what my brain was going through, but the bottom line was that my mind was working through the trauma. Today, watching Sean with his grandpa had shaken up some uneasiness and something inside me that had been more easily silenced during my time at school. Now, being out on my own with Emma with nothing to occupy that free space in my mind, I had noticed my thoughts and achy memories wandering back more than in the past, and my anxiety worsened.

When I told the story of what happened to them—the accident—I was not always sure what was true and what had been fabricated in my mind as a way of coping and pushing through the torment. The rest of my senior year was fuzzy when I thought back to it. But I did remember the whispers. Some people had stared at me sympathetically, and others couldn't even look at me. I imagined the conversations about me that they must have had behind closed doors. "Poor kid...to lose her whole family at the same time! Especially senior year." The voices never actually stopped. Emma and her family were my biggest—my only—supporters, but they still were not able to feel comfortable around me or to treat me normally. "I wonder how she will cope. She must feel so alone. Poor thing."

It was a drunk-driving accident, a combination of being in the wrong place at the wrong time and a night with fog so thick you couldn't see your hand in front of you. A game of If

Only was usually just a laundry list of things that had gone wrong, with not many ways they could have gone right.

We were celebrating my mom, who had recently passed her real estate exam, and we were driving home from dinner. Dad had made reservations at her favorite restaurant and had invited Grandma and me along. I had been planning on skipping out in true rebellious-teenager fashion, but an hour before we were due to leave, I got a phone call from Kyle Marsh, who had to cancel our plans.

Kyle had been my crush since third grade, the kind of crush so glorified that I could recall specific details of his little blond head and his denim overalls as he slid down the hot metal slide at recess and his sweaty palm in mine as we skipped down the hallway to get the milk for snacks for Mrs. Rodger's class. He had pressed a small yellow ring made of clay onto my pinky finger during the bus ride to the field trip at the apple farm. And then there was the day he flicked a triangular origami paper note at me in seventh-grade pre algebra. The scribbled mess of black ink read "Sup Cassidy. Math Sucks. UR2Cool. - Ky." And then the night he asked me to senior prom and I said yes.

When Kyle called, life as I knew it stopped, which was why I had been ready to ditch my mother's celebration dinner at the drop of a hat. I'd never really even thought of life without them. Some might say I didn't appreciate them when I could have. Maybe that was because I thought I had my whole lifetime left to be with them. How was I supposed to know that wasn't the case?

CHAPTER THREE

*E*mma and I ran into Sean and his grandfather a few more times over the next couple of weeks. Every single time was Grandpa's naptime, and he slept with his head down, United States Navy cap blocking his eyes. Sometimes he snored, and sometimes he was still. It wasn't until two complete weeks (but who was counting?) since our first encounter that while we sat on the sand as the sun went down in the distance, he opened his eyes for a brief moment, looked me squarely in the eyes, and smiled. I smiled back but not in time for him to see, as his heavy head fell forward again, his baseball cap drooping to the side.

It was that day in particular that Sean and I exchanged phone numbers and AOL screen names scribbled on the back of a gas station receipt that Emma had in her pocket. Mine was C@ssQuinn and his SurferBoy#1. We instant messaged and talked on the phone almost every day, and in mid-July, he pretended to high-five me but instead placed my hand between his and slipped a dark-tan hemp bracelet around my wrist, claiming to have made it on his own. Soon after that, I agreed to actually getting together without the company of Emma and Grandpa. After a few back-and-forth messages on the large PC that Emma and I shared in our living room, Sean and I decided to grab pizza downtown in York. I made him promise to avoid the Nubble, as I just couldn't be there on my night off, and he replied with, "Maybe, if you are lucky."

And lucky I was. It was the perfect night. He brought a blanket, and we sat on Short Sands Beach where the rocks met the first bit of hard sand when the tide started to go out. The pizza tasted just like I remembered it. Gran used to feed me so much of that pizza in the summer that Mom had to step in and intervene. But eating it here and now, with my toes in the sand and the stars in the sky and Sean by my side, was an entirely new experience.

"Now this is pizza," he mumbled as if reading my mind.

I nodded in agreement. "You can say that again." I laughed, knowing the second I said it that I would activate his goofy sense of humor.

"Now this is pizza," he mumbled again, laughing through his words.

"I haven't had this in so long," I replied.

"You've had it before?"

"Yes. I've spent a lot of time on the beach, and actually this beach from time to time." I closed my eyes and breathed in deeply, very much aware of the warm feeling that permeated me from the sea breeze and night sky.

"You haven't mentioned that before."

I nodded, placing my plate to the side and lying back on our blanket. I stretched my arms over my head and closed my eyes. "I guess there might be a lot you don't know about me."

He laughed and lay beside me. I noticed the heat from his arm, centimeters from mine. Our legs stretched out, and our bodies were parallel to each other. His pinky toe brushed against my awkward big toe.

"You used to vacation here?"

"My family used to take me to York Beach a lot. I spent hours climbing on those rocks as a kid. I used to dream that I lived in the Nubble Lighthouse."

"Lived there? Like in the lighthouse?" He smiled.

"Something funny?"

He shook his head. "I just think it's kind of cute."

"Well, I imagined it often. I used to pretend that I was a princess that lived on the top of it, kind of like Rapunzel. Waiting for my prince to come rescue me. It really feels like *so* long ago now."

He was quiet for a moment and then whispered a clumsy, "Used to?"

I gulped. Was that pity I sensed in his question? Curiosity? "Yes, used to. They died. In a car accident."

Usually, when I told this story, I felt as though I needed to make sure I was up to playing the part, portraying how traumatized and devastated I was, as if now that the information was out, I needed to display a sense of mourning. A smile would be a sin. But tonight, I said the words as if they were facts.

"All of them." I swallowed. "My mom, dad, and grandmother."

"All of them, in the same car?"

I nodded. "Actually, I was in the car too."

"For real?" he asked.

I wasn't sure if he realized he was holding my hand, but he was. I didn't want him to stop.

"For real." I pulled my hair off my forehead with my free hand to reveal the scar I had from the accident. "I'm still not sure how I walked away from it all with just this, but I did."

I turned my head to the left so that my cheek was on the

blanket and I was staring into Sean's large, round, dark eyes. The only reason I could even see them was because of the light from the moon, and the idea of that was so romantic that it was the icing on the cake of my whole existence and caused the tips of my toes to squirm and my insides to tingle.

"I guess sometimes I'm thankful I survived it, but in the same breath, it doesn't make sense as to why they would all be taken from me." I was surprised by the fluid way my words found themselves and how easy it was to tell Sean about my accident.

"Were you injured?"

I shook my head. "Just this scar." I thought for a moment. "I hit my head pretty hard, so I do still struggle with some memory issues."

"Memory issues?"

"Executive functioning is what they call it. I guess Grandpa and I have some things in common." I laughed.

"I'm so sorry, Cass," he whispered.

Cass. That was the first time he'd called me that. My fingers fiddled with the threads of hemp around my wrist, and as I looked into his eyes, I wondered if, ten years down the road, every time he called me Cass, I would remember this absolute perfect second: the moment the breeze from the Atlantic Ocean teased our senses with its salty air and gentle touch; when the light from the moon glistened just enough for our eyes to meet and for me to peer into his soul; when the sound of the crowds and the piano bar behind us quieted and slowed down just enough so I could hear his breathing and, I swear, the sound of his heartbeat.

Our eyes held a silent conversation that seemed to last ten years but was probably just ten minutes. At that point, we were so close together that I smelled the remnants of sauce from his pizza in combination with his peppermint gum, and my worries and fears for this moment faded. He gently held the side of my face, his pointer finger tracing my scar. An ache in my chest that I hadn't even been aware of went away. I closed my eyes, and our lips were together, and the rest of the world disappeared.

* * *

IT TURNED out that Sean was a great kisser—so much so, in fact, that we kissed practically everywhere we went. We kissed by the ocean during low tide, the sand surrounding us by what seemed like acres. We spent countless weekends with our bodies intertwined in the water, the smooth, rounded tips of gentle waves rocking us closer together, apart, and together again. We also made out in his car on my lunch break, parked by the rocks overlooking the Nubble Lighthouse, with nobody there to bother us aside from a few nosy tourists and pesky seagulls.

The best part about Sean was that he didn't seem to mind *just* kissing me. He kissed my face, my lips, my cheeks, my neck, and we lost control of our hands from time to time, but there was none of that pressure I had gotten from Kyle Marsh or some of the guys back in college. It was just enough. He was *more* than enough.

I also learned that not only could he carry a tune and rock on his acoustic guitar, but he also aspired to be a writer.

Alone time was hard to come by since he lived with his grandfather. Emma and I continued to work the breakfast and lunch shifts during the day and then hang out in the afternoons at the cottage or on the beach, so unfortunately for Emma, most of the kissing took place in front of her. She didn't seem to mind. Most of our years in undergrad had been spent with Emma placing a scrunchie on the doorknob to notify me that I would need to go chill in the lobby or do my homework in the library because she was somewhat, well, occupied. Emma had occupied herself very much during our four years together as college roommates.

I was thankful that she wasn't giving me a hard time about spending so much of my summer with Sean. She did, however, warn me that this just-kissing thing would only last so long before I, too, would need to start finding a place to "occupy" myself with Sean. She asked if I needed to borrow a scrunchie.

It turned out that Sean liked to drive with the windows down too. His explanation had to do with not wasting good ocean air. He said that Grandpa would never let him live it down if he turned on the air conditioning as he drove down the strip. I learned how to perfect the high ponytail for just that reason. Most of that first summer was spent with my ginger locks pulled up as high as their length would allow and completely sleeked back with my thick, stretchy white headband.

"Earth to Cassidy!" Sean joked.

"Sorry, I was spacing out, I guess."

"I'm just running inside to get my wallet, and then we can go."

It had been his idea for me to play hooky from the restaurant that Saturday morning. We were heading out for the day but needed to turn the car around for Sean's wallet.

"I don't understand why I can't come in." I placed his hand on top of mine and pulled it toward me. "I've never really met Grandpa awake, and I have *never* been in your cottage."

"Grandpa isn't really that nice." Sean laughed.

I kissed the top of his hand and looked up at him with puppy-dog eyes. "I don't care," I replied. "I want to see where you live. Besides, how bad can he be?"

I sort of already knew the answer to my question. When Grandpa had started to become forgetful a few years back,

Sean had started to worry. He would forget an appointment here or there or forget what he'd had for lunch. About a year after that, it got so bad that Sean quit his full-time job in construction and stayed at the cottage to act as his caregiver. The whole idea of Sean putting his life on hold to care for Grandpa, who was later diagnosed with dementia, only made me fall for him harder and faster.

I CLIMBED the tall cement stairs that led up to the second-floor porch of the three-story house. I had only really ever seen it from the front, on the beach side. The light-gray siding and white shutters were familiar; the only difference from my usual view were the white balcony porches that lined each level. It looked taller from this angle somehow.

Sean unlocked the door and poked his head inside. "Hey, Grandpa, my friend is here!" he shouted as we entered the sunporch.

"Friend?" I laughed. I playfully tapped him on his back. The humidity of the afternoon forced his T-shirt to stick to his skin.

"Listen, I'm not trying to define our relationship. It's just to make sure he is actually wearing pants—which, by the way, I can't guarantee."

The kitchen smelled like freshly cooked bacon and coffee with a hint of cigars. Large picture windows that overlooked the ocean encompassed each room. Sunlight beamed in from the shore, and there was no need for wall decorations or even curtains for that matter; the ocean served as any necessary decor. The antique furniture reminded me of my grandmother's house. I brushed away the dull ache that stirred inside my stomach. *If only.*

Grandpa sat in the corner of the living room on a brown-and-black-plaid chair with a navy-blue blanket draped over his legs and a newspaper sprawled across his lap. He grunted at the sight of Sean standing in front of him. He took a sip of coffee and looked up from the newspaper. "I didn't know you were here."

"Oh, sorry, Grandpa. I shouted for you when I came in."

"What did you say?" he shouted back.

Sean raised the volume of his voice so Grandpa could hear him. "I said I brought my friend to meet you."

Grandpa looked up at me, and his dark eyes met mine. His shoulders pushed back, and his voice caught in his throat.

"Grandpa," Sean said again and then looked at me as if to say "Told you so." "This is my friend Cassidy."

I extended my hand to offer my best handshake. "Hi. I'm Cassidy. It is nice to meet you."

Grandpa pulled back his hand and cleared his throat. "Dolly," he mumbled, his finger pointing at me. "Dolly…"

"I'm not sure what you are asking. I'm sorry."

He jumped to his feet, startling both Sean and me. The newspaper slid off his lap, followed by the blanket, and Sean had been correct—no pants. "Dolly…son of a gun." He waved one hand in front of his face as if it was some sort of magic wand, and the excitement didn't bode well for the mug in his other hand.

"Yes, Grandpa," Sean said, placing one hand on his shoulder while the other reached for the coffee mug. "You have met her on the beach."

The scene would have been almost funny if not for the look of worry in Sean's eyes.

"I know who she is," he snapped. Grandpa slammed his hand down, and the coffee mug followed, smashing on the tile and sending coffee spraying up onto all three of us. It was actually impressive that the small amount of liquid could do so much damage. Grandpa bent down to pick up the ceramic pieces, but I hurried to him and gently grabbed his wrist, worried that he would cut himself.

"Thanks," Sean muttered. "I'll get the broom."

I kicked the remaining shards out of the way with the side of my flip-flop, careful not to cut myself. Working with the elderly had never been my thing, but something reminded me of *her*, and I knew just what to do. I took Grandpa's other hand in mind and looked him in the eyes. They were melancholy but almost hopeful at the same time.

"It's going to be okay," I stated confidently.

His dark eyes softened, and he clutched my hand tightly. I helped him sit back in his armchair, thankful that although he had forgotten to put on pants, he had been in a clear enough state of mind to toss on a pair of underwear. My breath caught in my throat, but as I continued to lock my eyes with his, I realized my words of encouragement were not meant for just him.

I picked up the blanket and tossed it to the side, barely aware that Sean was next to me, sweeping up the glass. I noticed another blanket on the couch next to us and settled it on Grandpa's lap. "There you go," I whispered cheerfully. "Told you it was going to be okay."

Grandpa coughed. "Yes," he murmured. "Now that you've come back."

I stared at him in confusion. It must have been so hard to live this way. Trying to remember anything at all must have been hard, let alone trying to distinguish between what was real and what was not.

"Would you like another coffee?" I asked.

I was not sure if Sean was within hearing distance of that conversation. I heard the vacuum running next to us and confirmed he had not heard it.

Grandpa gently took my hand and placed it to the side of his face. His skin felt rough. He felt cold and a little bit shaky.

"I knew you would come back," he repeated. His skin showed his age, but his grin was boyish, almost as if he knew a secret or was up to no good.

I peered over my shoulder at Sean, who was now wiping everything up, and quickly pulled my hand back from Grandpa's. I decided that there was no need to bother him with any of this. He had enough here to deal with.

"How do you take your coffee?" I asked again, a bit more firmly this time.

SUMMER OF 2001- CASSIDY

CHAPTER FOUR

*T*he rest of the summer went by quickly. The more time I spent at the cottage with Sean and Grandpa, the more I started falling in love with both of them. Both were difficult at times. Sean mostly wanted to whisk me away for alone time (we were very occupied), and Grandpa had taken a very strong interest in me and always wanted me there one minute and was angry with me the next.

One Monday, I awoke sick as a dog, as Grandma used to say. My head was pounding so hard it felt as if it was being beaten with a sledgehammer. Emma and I didn't have a thermometer, but there was no doubt I was burning up. I *hated* being sick. It rarely happened, and when it did, I turned into a total baby and refused to go to the doctor.

By Wednesday, when I had only gotten worse, Emma called Sean for reinforcement. I begged him to stay away. Not only did I despise the idea of him seeing me like that, but I was nervous that I would get him sick and he, in turn, would infect Grandpa. By that Wednesday night, Sean had not only picked me up and taken me to the emergency room but organized himself actual shifts between Grandpa and me. I was diagnosed with the flu and needed IV fluids before being released back to the Seaberry.

As humiliating as it was for him to see me tired, sick, and weepy, I was unimaginably grateful just to have him there with me. At one point, I even let him come into the bathroom with me, and I sat with my legs scrunched up in our small cottage tub as he helped me wash my hair. My body shook involuntarily, and with every touch, my muscles tightened.

"This is so embarrassing," I sniffled between sobs.

He said nothing at first but rubbed my back with a washcloth.

"I want my mom," I wailed. It was something that I never actually said out loud. "Ugh, I can't believe I just said that out loud." And then I cried harder.

He helped me out of the tub and wrapped me in an oversized beach towel, pulling me close. "You have me. I am your boyfriend, and I'm not going anywhere."

* * *

THE FLU CAME AND WENT, and by some small miracle, nobody else got sick. Again, I was thankful for Emma, who was not at all dramatic about my new relationship and interest in helping Grandpa with daily tasks like making coffee, lighting his cigar, putting out his cigar, and of course, remembering pants. Emma actually insisted it was sweet that I'd found a way to channel my inner grief over the accident and was sure that taking care of Grandpa was my way of healing the hole I had in my heart for Grandma. It didn't hurt the situation, either, that Emma was making some new friends—mostly male—and was also spending her time with new people from new places. However, we continued our tradition of beers and sea glass every Friday at five p.m.

On this particular Friday, though, as we splashed our feet along the shore, keg cups in hand, I could sense that the water was already starting to get cooler. I knew it was mid-August and that our time here would be coming to an end soon, but at times like this, when my toes started to feel numb from the colder-than-normal low tide and the dunes became less crowded with tourists, it became reality.

Emma, who had already taken a trip home to buy her textbooks for her master's classes and, surprising to me, had already been in touch with her advisor about student teaching, seemed actually excited about the next season in her life. For me, though, the thought of leaving Sean and Grandpa to head back to the city just seemed wrong.

"When do classes start?" she asked as if reading my mind, as she often did.

"Right after Labor Day."

"Any news on your roommate?"

I shook my head and sipped my beer. I bent down to pick up a seashell with a hole in the top. "When I was little, I used to save the ones with holes."

Emma nodded. "I know. You and Gran used to make necklaces." She elbowed me playfully.

"Sorry." I laughed.

"You guys made me a bracelet once."

I nodded, rinsed the shell off, and stuck it in the pocket of my shorts. I took another sip of my beer, a bit embarrassed that my memory sometimes left a lot to be desired. "I've been in contact with the landlord, and I know I have a space, but no, I don't know who my roommate is."

"Are you sure you plan on going back?"

I nudged her arm playfully. "Of course."

"Do you have all of your paperwork in?"

I knew she was referring to my 504 documents, the plan that explained to my teachers what accommodations would be helpful due to the injuries I'd suffered. Julie, my therapist, would need to sign off on them. I had managed to get into law school, but the 504 documents for my condition would be critical for my success.

She stopped and became serious for a moment. "Cassidy, you have been working for this your whole life."

I squinted my eyes in confusion. "And?" *And you are throwing it away for a guy?* I thought.

"And I don't want to see you stuck feeling bad about it."

I nodded. She didn't need to say any more. It was clear what she was implying.

We continued walking. Grandpa's gray beach cottage glistened in the setting sun. They were not outside today. I wondered if maybe Grandpa was having another bad day. There had been a lot of those lately. We continued walking, making small talk about low tide, broken seashells, and just how fast time flies.

* * *

"ARE YOU SURE HE IS ASLEEP?" I whispered, referring to Grandpa. Last we'd checked, he was sleeping contently on his armchair in the living room. We had put his cigar out for him and made a dash for Sean's bedroom upstairs.

He nodded, turned up his CD player, and immediately began covering my forehead with kisses.

"Third Eye Blind?" I asked between breaths. "I love them."

He chuckled and nodded, tossing me down on his bed. I wiggled myself up onto my elbows, moving his pillow to the side.

"I love that you love music as much as I do," he mumbled.

His voice sounded raspy and heavy. I realized he wasn't

thinking about Third Eye Blind anymore, and neither was I. His hands were already on the sides of my spaghetti-strap tank top, reaching underneath and lifting it off. He tossed it to the floor. I hadn't worn a bra with it, and my cheeks immediately turned as red as my hair. It was clearly a surprise to him too, and I watched in awe as he morphed from a male human being into complete primal savage.

"Sean...I..."

He placed his finger to my lips. "No talking tonight."

There had been so much talking lately. Talk about me moving back to the city, discussion about leaving the Seaberry, questions about what this would mean for us. When would we see each other? Would long distance even work?

"I know," I said. "It's just that this is our last night together this summer. And it's happening so fast."

He stopped kissing me and pulled back, searching my face for answers. "Do you want me to stop?"

No...yes...maybe...

"No," I whispered. "I...I just..." A tear fell from the corner of my eye. I hadn't planned for that to be there. "I'm just not ready for this to end." More tears escaped my closed eyes. I cringed in embarrassment following this confession.

His hands were the strongest I had ever felt them as they gripped the sides of my tear-streaked face. *Now he knows what a disaster I really am.*

"Cassidy, I'm falling in love with you." His voice sounded more intense than normal, almost desperate. "Nothing is ending tonight." His fingers traced the side of my forehead, where the scar from my accident was still so defined. I had stopped covering it up when he told me it looked badass. He traced it with his lips, and my breathing grew louder than normal.

I struggled to form identifiable sentences. "It's just...this has been..."

His kisses wiped away my tears and traced my neckline, moved over my chest and to my stomach and back up again. My fingers grabbed into the thickness of his hair, and I pulled his head close to me, but no matter how hard I tried, it wasn't close enough. I inhaled as long and as deeply as I could. He smelled of summer, our summer. Drakkar Noir, Doublemint gum, Bud Light, and salt air...*home*. He consumed my senses in every way possible.

His fingers unbuttoned my denim shorts, and he slipped them down my legs eagerly.

"Besides," he moaned, pulling his white T-shirt over his head. As he exposed his chest, his muscular frame loomed like a statue over me. "Not to sound like a cliché, but we still have tonight."

I exhaled and pulled him on top of me, squeezing him tight to my body.

"So...cliché." My words came out in muffled, broken moans. I held my breath, squeezed my eyes closed again, and forced myself to believe his words. This wasn't the end. It wasn't just a summer fling. His hands were on my waist, and mine were on his lower back. His lips were on my neck and my ears.

Could we actually make it work? I ran my fingers along the top of his back and kissed him back hungrily. I repeated his promise over and over in my mind as if memorizing his declaration to me. *This isn't over. This isn't the end.* I had never needed anything else to be so true. And as I buried my face in his neck in an effort to muffle the sounds that escaped from my soul—new and unfamiliar sounds—I felt like the luckiest girl alive.

I would never forget that moment: the moment I fell totally and utterly and madly in love. I returned my face into the crook of his neck, a place I could stay forever. As if reading my mind, he squeezed me tighter. We were the only two people on earth. Us, and Third Eye Blind. The alternative rock band continued to serenade us from the black Sony stereo with "How's it Gonna Be." The lyrics whispered, softly but almost with a hint of sadness and gentle warning. How would things be without him?

PART TWO

SUMMER OF 2006

SUMMER OF 2006- SEAN

CHAPTER FIVE

G randpa always said that shoes would tell you anything you wanted to know about a person. The first time I heard him mention this, I was about 10 years old. My parents had already shipped me to the East Coast to live with Grandpa after the divorce and had moved on to start their new lives with other people. At first, I thought Grandpa was being sort of snobby with this remark. I had asked him why he thought just because a person's shoes were shiny and fancy that it made them good. He smirked and laughed a little.

Now that I was a grown adult, approaching my late twenties, I finally figured it out. As I slipped my feet into my Adidas sandals and looked at the one side of my left shoe that was starting to break in the middle, while the entire insole of the other was wearing away to nothing, I got it. Looking at these broken sandals, you could totally learn about me. Broken. Tired.

Don't get me wrong. Life wasn't horrifying. It just wasn't easy. Grandpa's wishes were to stay out of the nursing home and live at the cottage as long as possible, and I was doing everything, I mean *everything* in my power to make that happen. But it was hard. It wasn't just Alzheimer's disease anymore; it was his breathing. He wasn't getting enough oxygen due to congestive heart failure.

When Grandpa was still in a solid state of mind, he had sat down with a lawyer and worked some stuff out. During that time, he put in writing what his wishes were and were not. No nursing home. No hospitals. Nothing that would keep him living any longer than God's intentions (his words). So when the diagnosis came about, we shut down the idea of tests pretty quickly. I started every day over coffee and bacon, reminding him what his name was and who I was. Why add conversations about hospital rooms, medications, and tests on top of it?

He asked about *her* all the time, right up until he became nonverbal, a term I had just learned for the first time. Of course, I blew it with her. I wish I understood his freaking obsession with her. At first, I thought we could make it work. When I promised her that it wasn't a fling, I had really and truly meant it. But who really knows what the future holds? I had my hands full with Grandpa, and she had law school. Life just got in the way. If only she hadn't started talking about getting serious.

As my coffee touched my lips, it felt warm in comparison to the breeze on shore that morning. Man, it felt good to get outside. Cool water brushed against my toes and over my feet, trapping sand between my sandals and my skin. I had left Grandpa inside with the hospice nurse, Jacki. It was actually Jacki who suggested I get some air to clear my mind. I wondered if Jacki had noticed that I probably hadn't showered or shaved in a few days.

"It won't be long," she had said to me two weeks ago. This was coming from the woman who had mentioned two months prior that she didn't like to give timelines. She had said it as if she was reading a script on the first day we met. We had sat, looking out the window of the cottage, talking about Grandpa and what they could do for him here to make things less painful and more amicable.

"Why not?" I had asked. I wasn't trying to be a jerk; I was just really curious. If my grandpa was going to die and she was an expert in this profession, it just made sense that she should be able to give me something. Anything.

But she had just shrugged and said, "Timelines don't really help, because I guess we just don't know."

I nodded and said nothing. I just stared at her and noticed how her blue eyes seemed emotionless. I tried not to judge her. My grandpa was dying. We used to watch a cartoon, Grandpa and I, and I remember in that cartoon, the character would fall down a hole each time he entered into another one of his fantasies. That was me now: falling...falling...falling. But nobody could tell me where the bottom would be.

"I guess that makes sense," I had finally managed to mutter.

She nodded slowly, and the tight blond bun on the top of her head almost moved a little. Almost. Jacki was good at this. It must have been hard to talk to people about these things, I decided. She must need to build a pretty big emotional wall of defense and have a good poker face. How awkward would it be if she was emotional?

"And plus," I added in sort of a whisper, "these things can be subjective." *What did that even mean?* I decided to stop talking.

"Yes," she agreed without missing a beat. "Very much so."

I had reached out and taken her hand in mine. It was not something I meant to do, but I did it anyway. "Thank you."

It only took about two more weeks before I was sleeping with Jacki. I didn't need anyone to judge me. I was already judging myself. And the truth was, what did it even matter anymore?

I reached into my pocket and pulled out my sunglasses. The sun seemed foreign to me. It pierced my eyeballs like a jagged blade. I rubbed my temples with my fingers and then brushed the back of my head with my hand. *Too much*, I thought to myself. And it was. What the hell was I supposed to do now? Aside from the fact that I hadn't worked in years, Grandpa was really all I had. I had contemplated reaching out to *her*, but what would I even say?

The last sip of coffee healed a piece of my soul as it traveled down, and I decided I would head back to the cottage. I turned around, kicking up sand as I walked. A flock of seagulls swarmed overhead, and a gentle breeze tickled the back of my neck. Goose bumps ran rapidly over both my arms. I looked down at my feet and found the perfect piece of turquoise sea glass, probably the smoothest piece I had ever laid eyes on. I knew in that second, that quick freaking second, that he was gone. I continued back to the cottage at a steady pace, already knowing that my life as I had known it for decades would never be the same.

CHAPTER SIX

*M*y grandmother used to make a huge, overwhelming deal of first impressions. Maybe that was why, as I tucked my blouse into my pencil skirt and did my best to shimmy up my nylons, I thought of her. It was true: first impressions were very important. And I needed to make a good one, because this was my third interview in two weeks, and I had not received one call back. There were not a ton of job openings in my field at that moment, so any and all interviews were critical to me.

Luckily, I had earned some scholarships over the years, but the truth was that I would be paying back student loans possibly forever. Thankfully, I had built myself up quite the savings account. Waitressing during law school was almost impossible, but I had done it. And I finished quite successfully, actually.

But the market for attorneys who graduated specializing in family law was slim. And I was no detective, but I'd caught sight of some of the other candidates in previous interviews, and I hated to play that card, but I was pretty sure I was missing one important thing: a penis.

This last interview would be my final attempt before taking my mentor's advice and starting to apply for paralegal positions. I knew there was nothing wrong with getting my foot in the door somewhere, but come on! I had graduated at the top of my class.

"I can do this," I said out loud to myself as I took one last glance in the mirror before grabbing my iPod and shoving it into the pocket of my suit coat. My ginger locks were slicked back in a twist, and my makeup was on point. I had perfected the art of covering up the scar on my forehead. I nodded in approval at my reflection. I was ready.

I glanced down at my watch. Ready and early. The interview wasn't for another three hours. *That's okay,* I thought to myself. *It is better to be early.* I had planned on taking a cab instead of the subway, and traffic could have been an issue. But I decided it would be better if I chilled out for a moment.

I grabbed a bottle of water from the fridge, unscrewed the top, and drank, careful not to mess up my lipstick. I looked around my messy apartment and saw clothes tossed over the couch and dishes still in the sink. I thought about cleaning up, but I was already dressed for my interview. The mess could wait. I kicked my strappy heels off next to the couch and sat down, putting in my earbuds and resting my head back, careful not to mess up my hair. I grabbed my flip phone and stuck it in the other pocket of my jacket.

I flipped through my music library on my iPod, past Pearl Jam, past Lifehouse, and settled on Dave Matthews. Although Emma had always despised my choice in music, she really hated Dave—even more than Pearl Jam.

"When it comes to whiny," she had said, "Dave Matthews takes the cake."

I rolled my eyes at her and laughed. "Then what do you listen to, Emma?" I didn't even remember what she had said, but her answer was nothing remotely relevant.

I closed my eyes and tried to relax and control my beating heart. Why did I have to get so nervous for interviews? From the depths of my earbuds, Dave soothed me.

I jumped, my thoughts quickly interrupted by the vibrations of my cell phone in my pocket. I sighed. It was probably Emma. I pulled out one earbud and flipped my phone open, surprised to see a number I didn't recognize. It was not a Boston area code. I grunted in frustration, wondering who had gotten this number and what they were trying to sell me today.

"Hello?" I asked in my most annoyed "take me off your list" voice.

"Hello. Yes, is this Cassidy Quinn?"

I rolled my eyes and pulled out the other earbud. "Can I tell her who is calling?" I asked, trying to sound like a secretary.

"This is Molly calling from attorney Todd Michaud's office."

I paused for a beat, swapped my phone to the other ear, and waited for her to continue. Could this be a potential interview? *Oh man...crap...shit.* My thoughts ricocheted through my mind at the speed of light.

"Can I leave a message for her then?" she asked politely.

"No, that's okay. Please hold." I pressed my palm to my forehead and rolled my eyes. Staring up at the ceiling, I cursed myself for being so damn awkward. I cleared my throat and tried my hardest to change my tone. "This is Cassidy," I stated firmly and professionally.

"Hi, Cassidy. This is Molly calling from attorney Todd Michaud's office," she stated again.

I silently thanked her for playing along if she had in fact figured out it was me.

"Hi, Molly! What can I do for you today?" I grimaced, asking myself why I always came across so amateurish.

"I am calling on behalf of Gerald Anderson," she said.

Gerald? Anderson? I glanced down at my watch, careful not to lose track of time, as this clearly was not someone looking to hire me.

"I don't think I know anyone by that name." I admitted.

"Gerald Anderson of York Beach in Maine?" she asked.

York Beach? I jumped to my feet. *Anderson. Sean Anderson? Who was Gerald?* "I...uh...I know the last name, but it has been years."

"We are going to need to set up a time for you to come into the office."

"Office?" *Gerald? Grandpa? Was Grandpa Gerald?*

"Yes, the office of Todd Michaud," she said again, clearly beginning to lose her patience.

I haven't thought of that little jackass, Sean, in years, I thought, completely lying to myself.

"Molly, I, uh, I don't know what this is regarding, but I am in the city. Coming up to Maine right now is just not really good timing, you know?"

Molly didn't know, because her tone became firm. "I can get you in to see the attorney on Thursday or Friday of this week at ten a.m. if that works for you."

"What is this regarding?"

"I'm not at liberty to give you specific details over the phone, but it is regarding the estate of Gerald Anderson."

I hadn't realized it until then, but I had been pacing around my living room. I was now over by the window, overlooking the city skyline, one hand pressed to my phone and the other to the window. *Sean. Sean Anderson. Estate of Gerald Anderson.* It didn't take years of law school to put two and two together. Gerald Anderson had passed away —*Grandpa* had passed away. But what did this have to do with me?

"Friday at ten works," I replied with a sigh.

"I will put you in his calendar, and we look forward to seeing you then."

PART THREE

NOW

NOW- CASSIDY

CHAPTER SEVEN

I love waking up to his face in the morning. I love that moment when he isn't awake yet but I am. I can tease him for drooling later, or not. It is totally freeing, and I love it. And in one week, we will be married. Married! How did I get here? To this place in my life where I am an actual grown-up with a job and a fiancé? I don't know. It's a good question. They say it happens fast. But I didn't realize it would be *this* fast.

As if on cue, Colton opens his eyes. They are green, almost just like mine. He smiles and brushes his blonde hair away from his face. He needs to shave. "Was I drooling?" he asks with a laugh.

"No," I lie.

"Good." He pulls me close and kisses my forehead. "I can't believe by the end of this week, you are going to be Mrs. Freaking Pershing." His voice trails off as his lips move from my forehead to my nose to my lips.

I giggle as I pull away. "That is Attorney Freaking Pershing to you," I joke.

But seriously, I think. *Cassidy Pershing.* This is really happening? There is a quick moment of dread in the pit of my stomach as I think about letting go of my own name—my family's name.

He pulls me close, and I surrender, allowing him to continue kissing my ears and my neck. He pulls the strap of my nightgown off my shoulder and continues kissing. His lips and his breath feel warm against my skin.

"Attorney Cassidy Anne Pershing," he whispers into my ear.

I have to admit, it does turn me on. We have been planning this wedding for two years. You wouldn't think the idea of a name change would be great foreplay, but apparently it is.

His hands feel strong and steady as he grabs my waist and lifts me over him with little effort. I am wearing the nightgown he bought for me last Valentine's Day. It was really the first time a guy had ever bought me anything on Valentine's Day. Emma and I always called it a flaky Hallmark holiday, probably because we were bitter. Looking back, I see that now. Because now my legs are straddling the torso of my super-hot fiancé's fantastic abs, and my silky Valentine's nightgown is being pulled over my head. Hallmark holiday or not, I decide I don't care.

This continues for most of the morning. After all, it is Sunday, one of the last Sundays before we get *married.* If I get out of our bed, then I will have to face the fact that this massive event I have been planning for two years is almost here. And although I have every detail planned and all of the invitations have gone out and RSVPs have come back with i's dotted and t's crossed, it is still here. I would rather lie in bed with this man who is going to be mine forever and let him kiss me right…yup…there. *Colton…*

· · ·

WE FINALLY GET out of bed about four hours later because the delivery guy is buzzing for us to come down. Colton ordered greasy burgers and shakes, and I opted for an order of sushi with mine. It is perfect. It could possibly be like this every Sunday for the rest of our lives.

I'm not nervous about getting married. This has been planned now for quite some time. It took us a while to choose a venue, but when we did, we both fell in love with it: a quaint country club right outside the city.

It is going to be a big wedding. I obviously won't have much family coming, but Colton is the baby boy of five siblings, and his family is enormous. I wanted a small wedding party—just Emma. But Colton's mother, Doris, insisted that his siblings all be included. Therefore, my wedding party consists of Emma as my maid of honor and a whole lot of Pershings. There is Colton's sister, Amelia, who is older than he is by exactly thirteen months (way to go Doris), whose four-year-old twins, Drew and Dakota, will be my flower girl and ring bearer. Then there is also Colton's younger sister, Sophie, who just turned twenty-one. On Colton's side of the party, he has his best man, Michael, who is also his best friend from college, and his younger twin brothers, Landon and Nathan, who are bachelors in their thirties and very attractive. Emma has her sights on Landon but has already disclosed to me in confidence that on my wedding night, she will take whichever is the most single, the most available, and the most willing to keep her occupied.

So there it is. I have found my Prince Charming, and ours might as well be a royal wedding at this point. Everything is planned, down to my something old, new, borrowed, and blue. My something old is a handkerchief that used to belong to Gran, which I intend to hold in my palm around my bouquet of pink roses. My something new is a diamond necklace Colton surprised me with last weekend on my thirty-eighth birthday. My something borrowed is earrings from Emma that I have always adored. My something blue is a garter that I will wear on my thigh for tradition's sake—and because it is important for there to be a bouquet toss, and according to Doris, you need the garter for that. Tradition, tradition, tradition.

I hop back into bed and squirm under the covers. My down comforter slides easily along my bare legs, and I reach to the nightstand for my cell phone. This has turned out to be just what I needed: the perfect Sunday. I scroll through my past texts and message Emma.

Cass: One week! Can you believe it?
Emma: I can't!
Cass: When will you be in the city?
Emma: Friday. Last day of school is Wednesday. It's a half day.
Cass: You must be excited for summer.
Emma: Eighth graders are the devil.
Cass: LOL

"Hey, babe," Colton calls.
I glance over to the door of the master bathroom. "You need something?" I call back. He is always forgetting a towel. For such a smart and successful man, if he didn't have his head attached to his neck, I swear he...
"Yeah. You, naked."

Cass: TTYL :)

* * *

SATISFIED with my perfect last Sunday as Cassidy Quinn, I choose to curl back up in bed early. My head spins with thoughts and final details of the big day. I also can't wait to see my best friend. My family is basically Emma and Emma's parents. After all, they did raise me for an entire year. Emma's father offered to walk me down the aisle, but I declined, secure enough in my reality that I could do it myself.

I grab my laptop and pull it onto my lap. With Colton snoring and drooling next to me, I open my Google spreadsheet and check to make sure all is in order. Although I can't seem to find anything missing, I can't help but think that maybe I forgot something.

Annoyed with myself, I close out of the spreadsheet and open Facebook to take my mind off of it. I find it funny that some people have elaborate accounts extending back ten years, while others (Kyle Marsh and Sean Anderson, for starters) are absolutely nonexistent. I scroll through my news feed, glancing at posts of friends from work, old friends from school, college, distant cousins. I have 678 friends. Sometimes I wonder who these people are. I know there is some connection, but I sometimes cringe at the thought of calling them friends. They have cats, dogs, kids—kids in football uniforms, ballet tutus, and pigtails. These "friends" drink martinis and post pictures of their feet in sandals in front of tropical water.

I wonder, are they happy? Is this the happiness I have been chasing? I shudder at the empty, taunting ache in my chest and at the back of my mind. I close my laptop and tell myself that I am happy. At thirty-eight years old, I am happy.

I reopen my computer and click back on the post of Rachel Archenbault's magenta pedicure in front of the tropical sea and think to myself, *I am happy.* I am a little envious of that ocean water though. Sometimes I really miss the sea.

. . .

I WAKE up in the middle of the night, sick as a freaking dog. I almost don't make it to the bathroom before vomiting. I flush the toilet and crawl across the bathroom floor. This is bad. This is really bad. Dear Lord, am I pregnant? Is this what pregnancy feels like? The cold tile hurts my knees, and the room is spinning. What the hell is wrong with me? I immediately start self-assessing. And crying.

"Colton," I cry out. All I hear is snoring. Why does my fiancé have to be a heavy sleeper?

I grab a bucket and crawl back into our room but only make it a few steps before I realize that I need both the bucket and the toilet.

AT SOME POINT in the morning, when the sun starts to peek through the window, Colton's alarm goes off. He is more than surprised to see me lying on the floor of the bathroom. I feel like death.

"Cassidy, what on earth..." It takes him a moment to figure out what has gone down for the past eight hours, and he is not at all enthused.

"I'm sick," I sob. "I can't even keep down water."

Colton grabs a hand towel and immediately covers his nose and mouth. "It's okay. Stay calm," he says very matter-of-factly.

My face is streaked with tears. I have completely destroyed our bathroom and probably his image of me forever.

"Do you think it was something you ate?" he asks hopefully.

I throw my arms over my head in question and turn back

to the bucket I have been throwing up in all night long. "I... think...I have a fever," I say in between sobs.

He nods. "This is not good."

* * *

IT TURNS out that although my fiancé has a heart of gold, he has a sensitive stomach around bodily fluids. I tried to cut him some slack at first. The guy was getting married within the next week, and if this was the flu and we considered incubation time, the timing was not good on his end. But whatever I had was horrible, and I started to become nervous when Doris (yes, he called his mother to take care of me) suggested we go to the emergency room. Doris sent a car to take me to the ER so that nobody else in the family would become exposed.

"So close to the wedding, dear," Doris had said. "We wouldn't want to cause more panic than has already been done."

I had nodded in agreement but wanted to shout, "Aren't you forgetting something pretty damn important? I am the bride!" But I kept my bridezilla meltdown to myself.

So now I lie here in the hospital, Googling *Sushi food poisoning: is it possible to get food poisoning from sushi?* I didn't want to believe the doctors, but it sounds like that's what it is. Even still, Colton and the rest of the family have not come to the hospital yet today. I have been admitted for observation and tested for the flu. That came up negative, thank God. I have been sitting here by myself with not even a phone charger. I have one red bar left on my battery. And I miss my mom.

I decide to use the sixty seconds of battery power I have left to send as many texts as I can.

Cass: I'm at the ER. I think i'm dying
Emma: WTF?! Where are you
Cass: Beth Israel, phone dying. Bad sushi.
Emma: Give me an hour

Cassidy: Where are you
Colton: I'm in a meeting
Cassidy: I'm freaking dying
Colton: <Thumbs-down emoji>
Cassidy: Are you coming here? My phone is dying-

My screen goes dark.

NOW- CASSIDY

CHAPTER EIGHT

*I*t wasn't just the sushi incident. It was everything. Sometimes I think that our expectations of happiness are false accumulations of what we see on other people's social media. The ironic part is that the Instagram moments we view are just snapshots of other people's good days and glory moments, and we shouldn't be striving so hard to duplicate them. It's just too bad that it took me three years, a $40,000 loss in nonrefundable wedding expenses, bad sushi, homelessness, and a broken heart before I realized I was going about it all wrong.

As I stand in front of the familiar concrete steps and stare up at the gray three-story beach cottage, I know that this is the place I need to be. I need to start over. I promised myself that I would use this opportunity and this summer to decide what, exactly, I think happiness is. My therapist back in Boston used to ask me what I thought my truths and my happiness were, and I would stare at her blankly. *What is my truth? My happiness? Shouldn't this be obvious?* My truth is that it isn't so easy, because the happiness I want will never be my reality. I want my family back. That isn't going to happen.

And even if, after this "break," I decide that I want to be with Colton, it needs to be for the right reasons. Let's face it: he spoiled me. Money wasn't a concern in the very least, and he came equipped with the big family I never had. Everything with Colton was easy. Everything with Colton was safe. Then why couldn't I be happy?

"Are you ready?" Emma asks. My best friend stands behind me on the concrete steps with my rolling suitcase behind her and a duffle bag on each shoulder. She is helping me move into the cottage.

Tears well up in the corners of my eyes. I'm trying to be strong, but once I left my fiancé at the altar, being strong felt kind of selfish.

"Let's do it," I reply.

THE SECOND FLOOR of Grandpa's cottage has been remodeled and redecorated. I haven't been in any of the bedrooms yet, but it is obvious that whoever is maintaining the property has made an effort to modernize it. Joey, the man I spoke with on the phone, is in charge of the property next door, but by some kind of private arrangement, he helps with the first and second floors of this one too. According to Joey, nobody has resided here since Sean and Grandpa did; they have only rented out the space to tourists through York Beach rental programs and Airbnb. The first floor is empty, and he isn't sure who is living on the third floor. He hasn't seen Sean in years and works directly through a friend of Sean's grandpa, who handles the estate.

The estate. That was a shocker for sure. I'm not sure what I feel worse about at this moment, the fact that I just bolted from Colton and the Pershing family or that in almost fifteen years, I haven't taken advantage of the Anderson Cottage, which was without a doubt one of the most generous gestures of my life.

The cottage smells clean, as if someone just mopped the entire floor with Lysol and shined the counters and wood-work with Murphy's Oil. It might just be in my mind, but I swear I can still smell bacon, coffee, and cigar smoke. I glance around the room at the picture windows overlooking the ocean. The black-and-brown-plaid armchair is there in the corner, but what looks like a new black leather sectional replaces Grandpa's antique couch. It doesn't seem to fit.

"So," Emma says, running her hands through her short black bob. "How the hell did this go down?"

I take a seat in Grandpa's chair and put my face in my hands. I gesture for her to sit, and she does so on the black leather sectional, kicking off her sandals and making herself at home like she always does. I still feel weak from the bad sushi incident. Of course she would be confused. I never told anyone about the phone call that day in 2006 and what Grandpa left for me.

"So," I begin. "I don't know why. Or how."

"Enlightening." She chuckles.

I roll my eyes. "Seriously," I say. "I don't know why or how he did it, but for some reason, when Grandpa met with his attorneys about his estate, he asked them to honor a deal..."

"A deal he made with you?"

"No," I sigh. "It doesn't make sense, but it happened."

"What happened?"

"Grandpa left me this cottage, not like to own it but to rent. He left it in his trust. They said he was of sound mind when he put it in writing. I just don't know how that is even possible. I don't ever remember meeting him when he was of sound mind."

"So what kind of deal are we talking about?" Emma gapes at me with wide eyes.

I frown and hit her with a pillow. "Em, it isn't like that."

"Then what is it like?"

I stare out the window. It's low tide. The dark, flat sand looks as if it could stretch on for miles. A sailboat seems to be stuck in place in the distance, looking tiny in comparison to the surrounding waters. Tall sea grass blows in the breeze in the sand outside the window. Surprisingly, there are no tourists outside, just one lonely seagull perched on top of a piece of driftwood.

It has been years since I have been here, and yet it feels like yesterday. I spent so many years angry with Sean, and then I just wasn't. I think at one point in my life, I decided that there would always be a special place in my heart for him and Grandpa. And then I got that phone call, and it rattled me, not only because Grandpa had passed away but because accepting any kind of offer from that man just didn't add up. I guessed I didn't want to take advantage of him. And Sean...he was just a summer fling.

"Um, hello?" Emma whines.

I brush my hair from my face. "One hundred dollars for one hundred days." I sigh.

"Huh?"

"That's the deal."

"What the hell does that even mean?"

I rub my eyes and pull my knees to my chest. My black leggings are already starting to collect wool from the chair. I start picking it off as if it is the most important thing I will ever do.

"I don't know," I start again. "The lawyer said that there was a deal made years ago with someone, family maybe. He wanted to pass that on to me. One hundred dollars cash for one hundred days of rental. Apparently it is a deal that he is honoring from, like, a hundred freaking years ago or something."

"One hundred dollars for one hundred days," Emma repeats. She looks as if she is thinking, but she might be judging me for not acting on it sooner. There have been hot summer days in the city when I would have given anything to be sitting here on this beach. But instead, we were melting in the city or lugging beach chairs on our backs blocks away from a public spot.

"So you just never came here?"

"Right. I was busy. I was trying to find a job as a lawyer. I felt like legally, it wasn't good timing." I know she's buying none of it.

Emma chooses her words carefully, and something about her tone feels familiar. "It's just weird to me that none of this has come up sooner."

I glance at her blankly, out of words.

"Are you sure this wasn't something that may have been discussed? Like before your accident?"

"Of course not. I told you, I didn't want to take advantage of him. And that summer…"

"That summer broke you," she finishes for me.

"It didn't break me," I scoff.

"It didn't help you," she argues.

"The year I lost *them* broke me," I argue.

I can tell she immediately feels bad. She pats the cushion next to her on the couch, gesturing for me to come sit. I obey, and before I know it, we are curled up on the couch, staring out the window of Grandpa's beach cottage at the end of June—the beginning of the summer—somewhere I swore I never wanted to be again.

"It didn't break me," I respond again, wiping another tear out of the corner of my eye.

But she isn't wrong. That summer with Sean and

Grandpa was the first time I tried to move on from my tragedy and make something new of myself. And it back-fired, to say the least. Sean didn't even try to make it work. He never came into the city once. Stopped calling and even instant messaging at one point. Sent no emails.

"Maybe coming back was a mistake," I mumble.

"Cassidy," she says, "you just left your fiancé. You moved out of your home. Took a leave from your job."

I nod, thankful for the friendly reminder that my life is in shambles.

"Where the hell else would you go?"

She is right, and I know this. When I had the idea to reach back out to the law firm that called me that day, I was still thinking emotionally. It wasn't until the law firm put me in touch with Joey Chase that I actually thought I would go through with anything like this. Joey said that he knew about the deal and that if I were to contact him, I would take priority over any renters. He just needed a few days to get the place cleaned up, and it was mine. One hundred dollars for a hundred days. He had actually been laughing when I handed him the cash this morning. If I'd had to guess, I would say that he had known Grandpa and remem-bered him fondly. Nothing about this deal was a surprise to him.

Emma leans over and plants a small kiss on my forehead. "Beers and sea glass?" she asks.

* * *

EMMA DECIDES to stay with me for the first night in the cottage. Because I refused to go up into Sean's room, she takes it, and I stay downstairs in Grandpa's old room. She insists that the place has been redone, and I am going to have to go up there sooner or later. She also jokes that I wasn't the last girl in that bed, and I should get over it sooner rather than later.

However, because she left in such a hurry to meet me at the hospital in Boston, she never really finished packing up her classroom for the summer. She needs to go back and do that, along with some summer science research projects she had started with a few of her enrichment students. I have been thankful for her company, but since I am determined to sort out my life over this one hundred days, it feels nice to have some quiet.

How does one go about sorting out her life? Should I go to Walmart and buy a dry-erase board? Make a list of pros and cons? Start a diary?

I decide to try all of these things, and after spending well over the budgeted amount on groceries and life-organizing supplies, I leave all of my shopping bags unpacked and pour myself a beer. I confirm with myself that beers and sea glass can be a single-person activity when said person is going through a major life crisis. Which I totally am.

* * *

I KICK the waves with my toes as I walk and sip my drink, careful as I step over large rocks hiding beneath the hard sand. Where did I go wrong? I try to think back to the last time I was happy, and honestly, I can't even remember what that looks like. All I can see when I close my eyes and think of happiness is both of my parents playing with me and my grandmother swimming with me in the ocean, my small hands wrapped around her fingers as she pulled me over the small waves.

I was even kind of happy when I dated Kyle Marsh. I loved listening to his band jam out. Kyle had a full head of shaggy blond hair and looked like a rock star when he played his Epiphone Les Paul Sl electric guitar. He strummed away on it effortlessly and surrendered to the waves of emotion that tore through him when he performed at the local clubs on the weekends. I laugh to myself, thinking about the time he let me lead a song or two during a gig. I wasn't sure what made me happier, those moments when I felt on top of the world or the quiet ones in which the two of us sat perched on his twin bed in the basement of his parents' house, softly smiling at each other as he played a song he'd written just for me.

Those were happy times. And so were the moments when it was just me and my family. I remember my parents so clearly. My father took me camping in the backyard as a child. We roasted marshmallows over the campfire, and he told ghost stories. I would catch my marshmallow on fire just to watch him try and stay at ease long enough to extinguish the flame. He would pitch a tent and put out our sleeping bags and tuck me in for the night, knowing very well I wouldn't last any later than ten p.m. before running inside to the comfort of my bed. My mother would be waiting inside for us with hot chocolate, taking over for my father, who would return to the comfort of his fire with a Bud Light and a book.

So why did everything have to change? Why did they have to leave me?

Before I even realize it, my entire beer is gone, and I am standing alone, facing the ocean, the cold water numbing the tips of my toes and making them feel prickly against the hard ground. I want to scream. I want to cry. I want Colton...and I don't. I want to sprint into the ocean, dive into a wave, and never come out again. I can't remember the last time I was happy. But I sure as hell remember the exact point in time when I started being sad.

NOW- SEAN

CHAPTER NINE

I wipe the remaining sand off of my arms and snap my surfboard onto the roof rack of my Jeep. The waves were killer out there today—just what I needed after the text I got earlier this morning from Joey. I haven't spoken with Joey in two or three years. He was on a recurring payment schedule with Grandpa's trustee, and he just sort of, well, handled it. We agreed that the only time he would need to contact me would be if there was a physical problem with the York property or if there was an emergency. I guess I forgot that I also told him to call me if she ever took Grandpa up on his offer. Such a weird offer, man. What the hell was his obsession with her?

From what I understood, Cassidy never even signed any documents related to Grandpa's estate due to something about being afraid he wasn't in sound mind when he offered her the deal. So technical. So lawyer. So Cass. So what was she doing now? Why, after all this time, was she interested in the cottage? Joey didn't mention anything about other people being there with her. Did she have a husband? A family?

I'm not on social media. If I was, I would drive myself

nuts. I've thought about it. It isn't that I believe that I am too good for Facebook, Instagram, or any of the other platforms; it's just that there isn't anyone I really want to talk to. What would have been the point of taking off to Southern California years ago for a fresh start if I was constantly looking over my shoulder at ex-girlfriends and their Instagram accounts? I have also had the occasional female turn me down for dates because I wasn't online. Apparently a certain amount of Facebook stalking needs to take place before I am safe to sit with for a few beers. I don't get upset about it though. If they need to analyze me before meeting me, then it was never meant to be in the first place.

I like California. I live alone in an apartment that is minutes from the coast, and even though I have writer's block big enough to stop a tsunami from hitting the continent, I get by with my music and my online freelance work. That is why I didn't need that text this morning. I don't need any more distraction; what I need is inspiration. I have so many ideas for my first book that I just can't start the process. And there are days I wish Grandpa were still here just so I could light his cigar, watch him doze off, and help him put it out.

The exchange had been brief:

Joey Chase: Surfs up Cali boy. Hope all is well. I have news about Gerry's place.
Sean: Hey man what's going on. Everything ok with the house?
Joey Chase: Things are good. Wanted to give you the heads up that Cassidy Quinn accepted the deal. She's renting.

THAT WAS where my heart skipped a beat and I grew weak in the knees. I tried to take a few deep breaths, but the air in my lungs sort of got stuck. I thought I was having a heart attack. I guess panic attacks are similar but feel like heart attacks. Why did she have this effect on me? How could she after all this time? Sometimes I think it was because of the way Grandpa felt about her. Part of me carried that to the end.

The end. That was what it was. And this is my new beginning. I'm not going to let her mess that up. I actually have a date tonight. I scroll through my text messages as I buckle the seat belt and start my car. I need a distraction.

Sean: Thanks for keeping me in the loop. Need anything?
Joey Chase: Sure thing. Nope, got it covered.

I START to type "Thanks for getting her settled" or "Does she have any questions?" But I hit the backspace key and deleted it, filing it in the "don't need to know" area of my mind.

I rub my hands through the back of my hair and grit my teeth. Why would she be there now? After all this time?

I need to get out of my head. I pull my phone off the dash and open my texts again.

Sean: Hey Stephanie this is Sean. Sean from the gym.
Stephanie: Hey you
Sean: We still on for tonight?
Stephanie: I was counting on it.
Sean: See you at 7:00
Stephanie: Can't wait. Xoxo

THAT'S RIGHT. Moving on. Not looking back. Cassidy can have her one hundred days in my grandfather's cottage. One hundred dollars for one hundred days. How did I not know about that prior to his passing? *Leave the cottage to a stranger, Grandpa, because that makes so much freaking sense. Not the guy who took care of you till the end. It's fine.*

I won't be thinking about Cassidy tonight, that's for sure. I grab my phone again and quickly type before driving away from the parking lot.

Sean: Want to make it 6:00? My place instead.
Stephanie: Absolutely. Text address.

* * *

MY NIGHT with Steph goes well in the sense that we basically get what we are hoping for or, in both cases, what we need. I can tell she isn't looking to get to know me better or build anything long term, like so many other women my age are looking to do. After all, she gets to my place around 6:00 as expected, and we don't even have time to talk about ordering dinner before her hands are playing with my hair and teasing the skin of my shoulders under the back of my shirt. I have barely finished cracking open the beers before her arms are wrapped around my shoulders and her red lipstick is smearing my lips.

It wouldn't be gentlemanly of me to turn her away at this point. I mean, hell, obviously I want her. Her tan skin, long legs, and tight abs are the perfect distraction. I manage to take a few swigs of my beer before she pulls my T-shirt over my head and starts tracing her hands across my chest, completely taking control.

"Are...are you...okay with...this?" I manage to mutter between short breaths. We have met a few times, but this is our first date. We have never even kissed, and she is basically mauling me. Maybe she should be asking *me* if *I* am okay with this.

Her gaze holds steady with mine as she unbuttons her top, revealing lots of black and lots of lace. "Sean," she sings more than speaks. I rub my eyes with my fists, trying to hang on to any sense of self-control I have left. But she is slipping out of her clothes and standing before me in my kitchen, pulling me toward her, her backside pressed against the granite countertop.

I close my eyes. "Don't think," is what I think I say.

We never make it to my bedroom. The kitchen counter serves its purpose, as does Stephanie. She leaves shortly afterward, first drinking a couple of sips of my beer and turning down the pizza. I can't imagine a girl like Stephanie eats too much pizza anyway.

NOW- CASSIDY

CHAPTER TEN

The Diary of Cassidy Quinn

I WRITE the words on the cover of the one-subject black spiral notebook I picked up at Walmart. I write it in cursive, which immediately annoys me. Who writes in cursive anymore? I decide to open the notebook and ignore my insecurity and desire to put the pen down. I sit out in front of the beach cottage, just as Sean did with Grandpa that first time Emma and I stumbled upon them.

I love the beach. The quiet and stillness almost act as sensory deprivation but at the same time overwhelm my senses. I adjust my sun hat and peek once again at the paper and pen.

DAY #10

. . .

It has been ten days since Emma and I arrived at Grandpa's cottage. It was so eerie walking through that door. Even stranger sitting in Grandpa's chair and sleeping in his room. So...it is day ten, and I still haven't even been in Sean's room. What is wrong with me? We dated for one summer like a million years ago. He was a fling. Did I love him? Who knows. Yes...no...maybe? Have I really even been in love? I would hope that I was in love with Colton. I agreed to marry him...I almost married him. How could I almost marry a man that I wasn't in love with? And if I did love Sean, then why didn't we try harder? Today I went on Facebook for the first time since the separation with Colton. I made the mistake of scrolling through my news feed and reading the opinions of those who did actually attend our wedding. On Instagram, there was actually a picture of him at the altar with the hashtag #nobride #leftataltar #runawaybride. I wonder how many of the people at the wedding knew that I had never actually put on my wedding dress that day. That I knew the night before...days before...that I wasn't going through with it.

Love. Is it directly linked to happiness? Can you be happy without being in love? Can you love if you aren't happy? And if I am truly trying to identify the last time I was really HAPPY, should I be trying to figure out if it was the last time I was in love? In true Cassidy fashion, I am deciding there should be a list.

Times I was happy: (In chronological order...obviously)

1. *Grandma snuggling with me in her wooden rocking chair, her pink sweater softly brushing against my cheek*
2. *Mom pushing me on a swing*
3. *Gran singing "Somewhere Over the Rainbow" while I fell asleep*
4. *Dad teaching me to ride a bike*

THE HUNDREDTH TIME AROUND

5. *My dog, Luna*
6. *Kyle proposing to me with a ring made of Play-Doh*
7. *Meeting Emma. Third grade first day of school*
8. *Doing the talent show with Emma*
9. *Winning the three-legged race and getting a blue ribbon*
10. *Mom and Dad dancing in the kitchen*
11. *Gran bringing me to the beach*
12. *Beach pizza*
13. *Shopping with Mom*
14. *Listening to Kyle play his guitar*

I DROP my pen and realize I can't make it past #14. Does this mean that I can't be happy because Gran and Mom died? I know this can't be how my story ends. People grieve all the time. People get help and come out on top. And looking at my list, I realize that I do have a lot to be happy for. But if this is the case, why can't I move past it? I decide I will try tomorrow. I fold up my beach chair and drop my notebook into my tote bag. The sun is starting to tuck away behind a cloud, and it is getting chilly. I decide that tonight might be a good night for number twelve, beach pizza. Sand kicks behind me as I make the trek back to the cottage, hopeful that tomorrow I can find my number fifteen.

DAY #15

I FEEL like I need to start this entry "Dear Diary." As a thirty-eight-year-old, I can't bring myself to do it. Maybe that's why I haven't written in a few days. The concept of having a diary seems so childish—no offense to you, diary. It's just that I am going to be old and alone. I just know it. I find myself these days missing my therapy sessions with Julie. I suppose seeing her for so long right after the accident made talking to her easy. I never felt judged by her. Maybe when I get back to the city, I will see her again.

Things have been pretty calm around here. I met a man walking his dog yesterday. The man is Sam, and his dog's name is Pete. Pete is a golden retriever. Sam is married and has children my age. Apparently they will be visiting this summer, and I will be meeting them.

I've been spending a lot of time in the cottage, cooking and baking. The baking part is hard because, well, who really wants to heat up a beach cottage with an oven in July? Most of my family recipes are in storage. The cooking that I do is from memory...or I look on Pinterest if I want to try something new. I am thinking of taking a trip into town for either a slow cooker or an Instant Pot. The tough part is I end up with a ton of food left over. I really am only cooking for myself.

Instead of trying to figure out #15, I have decided to skip #15 and move on to #16. This way, I can accept the fact that losing my family was the worst thing that could ever happen to me, wallow in my sorrows, and think about things that have made me happy since then. I decided, after careful consideration and a few glasses of wine, that this is what I am doing. Now, diary, I should warn you, I am four glasses in, and I need to go on record that I am in no way moving on from the tragedy. I am simply skipping over it. I have already broken out the cookie dough ice cream, and I'm not afraid to eat it if this gets worse.

Times I Was Happy List (continued)

15. SKIP
    16. High school graduation
    17. College with Emma
    18. College graduation

THE LAST DROPS of wine trickle out of my glass, and I toss my pen across the room. I close my notebook and crack open the cookie dough ice cream. That's enough for tonight.

* * *

DAY #20

DEAR DIARY,

See, I am getting better at that. The past week has been fantastic. I have finally settled in around here and have established a little bit of what I could consider a modified routine. Not a real routine, because I don't have any huge responsibilities or anything like that. But a modified routine, because I feel like I am doing what I came here for. Trying to figure out what makes me happy. And...I thought of another one! Helping people makes me happy.

So earlier this week, I was taking a walk, and I was on my cell with Emma when I decided to cut out back to pick some weeds under the steps that I noticed were growing up through the rocks in our parking spaces. I noticed an older woman lugging a huge load of groceries up the concrete steps, and she was struggling, the poor thing. I grabbed the bags from her, and you would never guess where she was renting from? The third floor of Grandpa's cottage. She had been living above me the whole entire time, and I had no clue. Her name is Emiline, and of course the first thing I told her was about my best friend Emma. She got a kick out of that and invited me up to the third floor for tea. How cute is that? TEA! It was like being in a movie. And to top it off, she is the cutest little lady with the sweetest British accent. I am in love with her.

Emiline is in her seventies, and she has been renting off and on from Joey for a few years now. She said that the cottage is typically quiet, as Joey spends most of his time in Wells, but she loves coming in July, because her grandchildren live in the States, and they come to join her. She hoped I wouldn't mind some children being around in the coming weeks. I told her I love kids...I started to tell her about Drew and Dakota but changed the subject quickly. She didn't need to know I left my fiancé at the altar just yet.

I asked her if there had been other renters on the first and second floors, and she explained that yes, the second floor is rented often, but not the first. She told me that the brass key on my ring (I wondered what that was for) was so that I could go down to the basement and either store what I needed to or borrow beach equipment. I wonder why Joey didn't share this with me? I plan on heading down this week to check it out. I also asked Emiline what her favorite thing to eat for supper was...and you know what she said? Meatballs! I went into town and bought an Instant Pot so I could make Emma's meatball recipe, and I will bring some up to her tomorrow. So long story short, I found two more for my list.

22. Helping people
23. Making friends

I SIGH and tuck my notebook into the drawer under the counter and continue to unpack my Instant Pot. Emma promised to talk me through how these things work. But for now, it will be a YouTube tutorial. I heard you can make meatballs in this thing in twelve minutes exactly. Hallelujah. Now if I could only insta-fix my life in twelve minutes. How about a time machine? Hopefully I don't burn the cottage down making this recipe.

NOW-SEAN

CHAPTER ELEVEN

I've made it my entire lifetime without actually showing up at a high school reunion. It's not that I didn't like high school; it's just that I never really felt connected enough to see anyone or go through the process of putting on a button-down in an effort to impress strangers. Plus my five-year and ten-year reunions were tossed together as Facebook invitations or email invites and were just local bar hangouts. This came to my apartment in the actual mailbox, and that is probably why I didn't throw it out back in April.

I thought the summer was a weird time to have a high school reunion, and I mentioned this on the reunion link I used to RSVP. First, I checked the YES box to confirm that I would be in attendance (it is insinuated that I will be bringing a guest even though I probably won't), and then I had to choose between steak, chicken, or vegetarian. Did I have any food allergies? I checked NO and the same for my alleged guest then clicked submit. After doing so, I was bombarded with past messages and texts from the group and comments from the planning committee. It appeared as though this had been in the works for some time now. There was even a survey. *Please click on the date that works best for you!* Heart emoji, smiley-face emoji. The planning committee was very cheerful.

This answered my question about timing. Summer beat out late spring by at least forty percent of the votes, because it turns out I graduated with a lot of classmates who became teachers. After being exhausted through the dialogue and funny memes my graduating class seemed to believe to be entertaining, I learned that most everyone just needed this event to be at the Union Bluff Hotel and Event Center. I submitted my fifty dollars through Venmo and clicked past the opportunity to submit pictures. And now here I am, on a plane back home for my twenty-year class reunion.

I didn't even bother to check luggage. I have everything I need in my backpack and figure I can pick up a sport coat back home. My neck is stiff from the flight, and I stare at the blank screen in front of me. Still blank. Still no ideas. I was hoping for some inspiration by now, but what I think I need is a reset. A high school reunion could definitely spark some interest and maybe inspire some creativity. Then again, so could the East Coast, and so could...well, we will see if she is even interested in speaking to me.

"Ladies and gentlemen, we ask that you please take your seats and observe the seat belt sign, as the captain has reported we will be making our way through a bit of turbulence before our final descent."

If nothing else, I think, *I have learned to deal with turbulence.*

* * *

BY THE TIME I land in Manchester and Uber up to York, it is about three a.m. I am exhausted. I thank the Uber driver and grab my stuff, welcoming the comfort of the slight chill in the night air. I also realize, as I get out of the car, that I am beyond starving. I am relieved that I still have some airport snacks in my backpack, as literally nothing will be open until morning.

The lights on the second and top floors of Grandpa's place are off. I am irked that Joey rented out the second floor to Cassidy and not the first. I feel like I am home but can't actually go *home*. The first floor will have to do. Joey left me keys underneath a plant downstairs, and I drop my bag off the side of my shoulder, knocking over another potted plant to the side of me as I search for them. I grunt in frustration and finally locate the keys. Then I slide them into the door-knob and push the door open with my hip.

Wow. Joey has done a really nice job with the place. It has been years since I've been home but even longer since I stepped foot on the first floor. I remember it smelling moldy and musty, but not anymore. The wooden bar that Grandpa made by hand is still there, set off in the corner of a small den. Two black leather recliners face the original fireplace. The red bricks have been painted white. A small table with two placemats rests in the corner of the kitchen. The counters still need updating, but the floors are new. I am happy to see they have been replaced by white ceramic tile that's way more practical than the carpet that was here before.

The windows on this floor are tiny in comparison to the ones on the second floor. I barely turn on any lights as I make my way to the bedroom. I'm impressed again at Joey's ability to keep this place up at his age. That dude must be one hundred years old by now.

I don't even use the bathroom or change my clothes. I drop my body on top of what feels like an afghan or a quilt, and I am too exhausted even to remove my shoes. My thoughts are fuzzy and scattered, covering everything from *I think I had my first kiss in this room* to straining my memory in regard to my childhood and my reunion. Who will I even remember? What am I doing here? Will I see Cassidy tomorrow? Will she come with me to the reunion? Is she even single? At this point, I will consider myself a lucky man if she doesn't punch me square in the face. I would deserve it.

* * *

I WAKE up to the sun blinding me through the blinds I didn't think to close. I rummage through my backpack for my toothpaste and my shower stuff but quickly realize I don't need most of it. Joey has this place stocked with everything I could need. I can see what Grandpa loved about him.

It feels good to shower, but man, I am starving. In the kitchen, I find everything I might need to cook but no food. Not even coffee. My Apple Watch tells me it is nine fifteen, definitely late enough to head out and get something, but I'm running out of time to prepare for the reunion. I don't have time for groceries.

"Hey, Joey, I'm back. Do you have any eggs I can cook or some coffee?" I ask into my Apple Watch.

"No, but the girl renting the second floor has been cooking up a storm. You could always go up there," he texts back.

I cringe and rub my hands through the back of my hair.

Cass.

THE WEST COAST IS BEAUTIFUL, but there is just something about New England. The sand feels thick and grainy on my bare feet as I hop up the porch steps to the second floor, just as I have done so many times before. My hands are a little sweaty and shaky as I knock on the storm door. It feels awkward that I can't just walk into my own house.

I hear quick footsteps, and I step backward, both surprised and a little overwhelmed when a little girl with blond pigtails peeks through the screen. *I knew it. I knew she has a kid. I'm such an idiot, to think someone else wouldn't scoop her up. If only...*

"Is someone there?" Cassidy calls from inside the cottage. Her voice is so familiar but yet not.

"It's a man! Stranger!" the little girl squeals and runs back into the cottage.

Adult footsteps approach the door, and I take a deep breath, ready for whatever happens. I notice the engagement diamond on her left ring finger before she even opens the door completely. At least I have an excuse to be here. Coffee and eggs. Coffee and eggs.

NOW- CASSIDY

CHAPTER TWELVE

*T*he first thought that goes through my mind as I watch little Jenny run back inside the cottage is, *I can't let someone else's kid get kidnapped.* The second thought I have is, *What in the actual hell?* Followed by *Thank God I brushed my teeth.* Because I most surely didn't brush my hair or change out of my pajama pants.

"Sean," I state as if I am swearing under oath on the witness stand.

"Cass," he whispers.

He's not surprised. He knew I was here.

"What are you..."

"I just flew in," he says. Peeking over my shoulder, he adds, "I'm starving. And Joey said you might have a couple of eggs..." His voice trails off too. "But I can come back. Your family...you're busy...it's totally cool." He puts his hands up, surrendering to whatever this is. It reminds me of the afternoon we met on the beach, a distant memory that's fading fast.

We stand here in the doorway. Jenny is behind me, giggling at my reaction to the man at the door. She is dressed in her purple-and-pink My Little Pony two-piece bathing suit. I'm taking her swimming this afternoon. Jenny...holy shit, he thinks she's...

"Jenny isn't mine," I blurt. I'm so awkward. *Stop talking,* I think.

He does a terrible job of hiding his relief. His eyes are the same eyes. His face is tan. His hair is the same hair. His hair...well, he has less than he used to, but it's a good look. Sean, at my freaking doorstep—well, his freaking doorstep.

"She's not?" He laughs.

"No. Jenny is Emiline's granddaughter."

"Emiline?" he asks.

I stare at him. For someone who looks the same, he isn't acting like the man I knew. The Sean from years ago would know who was renting Grandpa's third floor. I pull my hair behind my ears and close my pink sweater over my tank top.

"Come in," I sing as if I'm Bob Barker on *The Price Is Right,* inviting him to come on down!

"Are you sure?" he asks. "I don't want to…"

"Sean," I interrupt. "It's fine. Just come in."

HE MOVES awkwardly around the living room, and I can tell he is struggling to keep his attention on me while scoping out the place. I realize, as I capture moments of his curiosity, that I know just as little about him as he does about me. I giggle to myself but get some satisfaction from his reaction to sweet little Jenny, who took to me the moment we were introduced. She has been quite the positive distraction over the past few weeks—just what I needed.

"How has your summer been?" he asks, clearing his throat. He pulls a chair out from the kitchen table and sits down. He props his elbows on the surface.

The familiarity of his biceps and his posture and his mannerisms distracts me for a moment. How, after all this time, does someone pop back into my life, and parts of my brain and body remember things about him? As I rummage through the fridge and grab the eggs, I silently picture a filing cabinet in my brain with a file titled "Sean Anderson Summer 2001" being dropped suddenly and all the papers flying everywhere around me. And then I drop the egg.

"Shit!" I cry out. Then I'm embarrassed that Jenny has heard this and giggles more.

Sean jumps up and finds the paper towels and bends down next to me to clean it up. My cheeks are instantly warm, and I know my face matches the color of my hair.

"I only need a couple," he says. "I can take them with me and cook them downstairs. Maybe just a cup of coffee if you could?"

I stare at him wide-eyed. Is he serious? "Sean, I'm not sending you downstairs with raw food. Just sit down. How do you take your eggs?"

My exploding Sean file instantly screams *Over easy with toast, and his coffee is black*, but there is no way that his preference will be the same. I don't know this man anymore. Jennie was right. He is a stranger. Stranger danger. I quickly calculate the years since I last saw him, and when I realize how long it has been, I gasp. Twenty years? I wash my hands in the porcelain sink and dry them on the legs of my pants.

"Over easy would be good. You don't have any toast, do you?"

I make an effort to keep a straight face but know I am failing hopelessly. "Of course I do." I smile, trying to be chill. I am anything but. "I picked up a Keurig, so I have a bunch of different K-Cups if you want to look. I have cream and almond milk."

"Just black is fine." He is smirking. I swear he is smirking.

"Black it is then."

His eggs seem to take forever to cook. He is watching me. But he is also looking around the place like a detective. Is he thinking of Grandpa? Is he noticing the updates and the remodel? He is probably doing just what I did the second I walked in: appreciating the new but craving the old.

I manage, "It's been a while, huh?" with my back turned to him as I stand at the stove.

He sighs almost in relief, but I can tell he still feels uncomfortable. His eyes now fall on Jenny, who is scribbling in a *Paw Patrol* coloring book I picked up for her yesterday afternoon.

"This puppy is pink and purple," she announces proudly to Sean.

He laughs and seems to relax a little. "Oh yeah?" he asks. "What's her name?"

Jenny stops coloring and looks up at him, her tiny blue eyes squinting and her nose scrunching up in confusion. "How do you know it's a she?"

"Well," he says, "I guess because of the colors you chose."

"Boys can wear pink, silly," she explains. "But her name is Cassidy."

"That," he states with confidence, "is the most beautiful name I have ever known."

* * *

DIARY OF CASSIDY QUINN
   Day #38

SEAN. Freaking. Anderson. Are you kidding me? I feel like there should be hidden cameras and people jumping out and being like, "Hahaha, gotcha!" What was that show called? Was it Punked?

Anyway, diary, to say we ended things on bad terms would be the understatement of the century. We ended things on horrible terms. We didn't even say goodbye in person. He never even came into the city after that summer, and I never came back up north. What the hell?! We had this weird version of a breakup that was both phone and text, and he was drunk and I was overwhelmed, and we just never ended it right. And then there was that weird deal, and I thought Grandpa had been messing with me, and now I don't even know what to think.

This morning when I saw him, all I saw was him. I didn't see twenty years, I didn't see broken promises, I didn't see a failed relationship. I saw him. I was transported back in time to that summer. How, after this long, can I have these feelings? I would be kidding myself if I tried to say he wasn't feeling the same way. I swear he was flirting with me at one point. And to see him joking with Jenny, it was the cutest. But this dance we are doing? I can't help but feel guilty. What about Colton?

We didn't talk much, but I did agree to a walk on the beach tonight. Just to catch up, he said. Part of me doesn't even want to catch up. These past few weeks have been so great in terms of moving forward and letting go. How can I let go when my past shows up at the door?

* * *

It ends up being a gorgeous night. The beach has cleared of the late-July tourists, and the sky is beautiful in color. We have been walking nearly ten minutes now and have both been quiet. It is awkward not to hold his hand. I'm trying to play hard to get. It is possible that he is actually more attractive after fifteen years.

He speaks first. "I like your hair like that."

It is a simple statement, but I am thankful for the icebreaker.

"Oh." I laugh, trying to act as though his comment means nothing. It means everything. "Thank you." My red hair is pulled loosely back in a braid, my blond highlights peeking through. "Jenny's mother, Olivia, is a hairdresser. She did the blond highlights last week."

"Sounds like you have made some friends here."

I nod. "Yeah, I suppose I have."

"Are you still in touch with Emma?" he asks.

I smile. "Of course."

Our heads turn, and we both chuckle at the awkwardness of the moment.

"This water." He shivers. "It's freaking cold!"

"What?" I gasp. "It is not." I have gotten so used to walking on the shore this summer that I have practically forgotten my feet are even wet. "Where have you been living? The desert?" I bend down to grab a piece of sea glass, crystal clear and smooth, and stick it in my pocket.

He turns to me and playfully taps my arm, reminding me once again of that first day on the beach. The way his lip curves up to one side, his shy boyish grin, takes me back to that summer. "Southern California," he explains. "I moved out there after Grandpa..."

"I'm sorry about Grandpa," I say quietly.

"He was sick. It was expected."

"He was special," I argue. "It must have been awful."

Sean stops walking, and I do too. We are standing close together, but it feels too far apart. Studying his face, I can see it in his eyes. They are tired. They have surrendered. It's a feeling I have come to know too well.

"Cassidy, I'm really sorry. I'm really sorry about how we ended things."

Without realizing it, I turn my head away. "It's fine," I say.

"No," he counters. His voice is deeper, determined. "It's not fine. You deserve better than that."

"You were drunk that night. I shouldn't have been such a bitch about that phone call."

"You were not a bitch."

The desperation in his voice is so unexpected that I don't even realize that his hands are holding mine. We're silent again. The ocean wind tickles the back of my neck, and I shudder. I release my right hand from his and start to pull back. He is still holding my left hand in his. He is studying my engagement ring. His eyes meet mine.

"There is a lot you don't know," I say. "So much has changed. It's been so—"

"I know that," he interrupts. "And I'm not asking for a thing in return. I just want to apologize."

I nod but still feel uncertain. I feel regretful about so much that I didn't even realize it until now. I start to feel horrible about the way we left things. I feel even worse about not acknowledging Grandpa's death or the offer about the cottage.

"Is that why you came back here?" I ask.

He laughs and rubs his hands over his face. "No." He sighs and laughs again.

"What is it?"

He rakes his hands through his hair. "My high school reunion."

I burst out laughing. This is the last thing that I expect him to say. "Sean Anderson at a high school reunion. Alert the media!"

He smiles in return and kicks the sand up around us then playfully tickles my side. *He is totally flirting.*

"Stop." I giggle. I kick some water up, and it spatters his gray T-shirt. The sun has set, and dusk is setting in. But I am laser focused on one thing, and somehow, between an inhale and an exhale, I see nothing but the way his damp T-shirt makes areas of his chest muscles peek through. I am consumed by the scruff on his chin that wasn't there before.

All of this distracts me, and before I can muster any strength at all to thank him for this night and head on home, I cave. I let go and release control over whatever is happening. I bend down and grab the biggest, wettest palmful of sand and whip it playfully at his waist. I start to jog away, but he grabs me and tackles me, and we are both lying on the cold, hard ground. Chilled water seeps through the waist of my shorts, but I am so distracted by Sean—by all of this—that nothing seems to matter. We seem to be instantly connected, instantly us. Two days ago, I was preoccupied with dinner recipes and babysitting Jenny, and now I'm pinned down by a man, *this* man, who has vanished from my life for what feels like a hundred years. But here we are.

"Sean!" I exclaim in surprise as he lifts me off the wet ground with little effort.

We move up the hill onto softer sand. We are filthy. Have I lost my mind? I don't even know this person anymore. My mother used to say that there are certain people you could go without seeing for years and pick up right where you left off. Is that what is happening now? I was pretty sure I forgave Sean years ago. We were just kids, for crying out loud.

I laugh when I see how much beach sand we have both accumulated on our clothes. We are acting like children. My eyes meet his boyish grin, and I can't help but giggle like a five-year-old. I feel light. I feel giddy. I feel free.

He is propped up on his elbow, and his body hovers over mine, close enough that I can hear his heartbeat. I've been here before. And suddenly I'm not afraid.

"You know, Cass," he says, "there aren't many girls like you in this world."

I roll my eyes. "Yeah, okay."

He laughs. "Yeah, I know how it sounds. But it's true. I don't know what you have been up to for the past…"

"Fifteen," I say. "Fifteen years."

"Wow." He cringes. "I know things are different. I don't know why that ring is on your finger. I don't know why you chose this year for Grandpa's cottage."

I want to ask him if he knew about the deal. I want to ask him why, if I am so freaking special, has he never reached out? If there are really no other girls like me, then why didn't he come find me? Why couldn't he be bothered to Google me or reach out on Instagram? To call? He could have called. He could have texted. He could have done anything. *If only.*

I don't answer, and he studies my face. I am lost in him.

"Cass," he whispers.

I wait, wondering how this got so serious so fast, and suddenly I am nervous again. I brace myself for his next words.

"Will you come to my reunion with me?"

I burst out laughing and punch him playfully in the shoulder. I am laughing so hard that tears form in the corners of my eyes.

"Why are you laughing?"

I wish I knew, but I don't. I am out of words. I don't want to ruin this moment by talking about it. Something inside me doesn't want to know the answers. I don't want this to end. This feeling in my chest is warm, and my stomach is flip-flopping. I haven't felt this way in years.

"Yes." I laugh. "I'll go to your stupid reunion." And the joyful, happy, carefree me plants a huge, sandy, sloppy kiss on his perfect lips.

He exhales with what sounds like relief, pulls me on top of him, grabs my face, and kisses me again. Everything about him is warm. His arms are strong. He pulls back and wipes sand off the side of my face with his free hand.

"Good," he states with a smirk. "Because it's tomorrow."

"Tomorrow?" I want to punch him again, but I can't, because I need to kiss him. "What are you thinking?" I ask him in between wet, sandy kisses.

He sits up and lets my legs wrap around his waist. He kisses my cheek and the side of my ear and back to my lips. The heat from his torso feels warm between my thighs.

"I think," he says, kissing my nose and then cupping my face in his hands, "it's good to be home."

NOW- SEAN

CHAPTER THIRTEEN

*I*t was hard to sleep last night knowing that she was lying right above me on the second floor. She told me that I could stay, but I knew that this was the right thing to do. Good God, I can't remember the last time I wanted something, someone, so badly. But I can't screw it up this time. I messed it up big-time last time, and I won't let it happen again. I'm trying not to think about her engagement. I try not to think about her in someone else's arms. *What the hell happened to you, Cassidy? You deserve better than whoever he was. You deserve me. This time I will do it right.*

When I saw her yesterday, *damn,* I could see right through her "pajama" pants. That was what she called them. I can think of some other names for those pants. I'm pretty sure the devil himself invented them. It took all I had to play it cool. She looked the same, maybe even better than I remembered if that is possible. I don't know what is going on with her engagement, but I swear on all that is holy that I am going to scoop this woman up before anyone else has a chance. I'm a gambling man, but I'm not screwing around with Cass.

I check myself out in the mirror. I've pulled off a pretty good look in a short amount of time: a tan sport jacket with a white button-down, top button obviously open. I don't wear ties. Dark jeans. I hadn't noticed my tan until Cass pointed it out to me last night. She said I look like a California boy now. She isn't wrong. My hair is lighter than it has ever been. I've hit the gym and the waves more in the past couple years than I did in my entire life before. I've only been back east a couple of days, but I do miss those waves. As much as I love everything about the New England coast, the swells back west are mountainous compared to what we get here.

I'm satisfied with my reflection. I haven't been this clean-shaven in probably an entire decade. My face feels smooth. I wonder to myself what her face will feel like against mine.

I check my watch. I'm right on time to pick her up. I grab the bouquet of flowers from the counter and tuck my phone into my pocket along with my wallet. I grab my keys and lock the door behind me.

* * *

CASSIDY LOVES THE FLOWERS. She is blown away that I remember her love for sunflowers. Her face lights up like a kid's on Christmas Day. I wait while she fills up a mason jar from Grandpa's cabinet and carefully places them in there, admiring them with a smile. She looks amazing. But seriously, when does she not? Her dress is tight in all the right places, and it is not long. It's shorter than anything I have ever seen her wear before, anyway. The neckline doesn't leave much to the imagination. Not that I need to imagine; I remember every detail about her.

"You look amazing," I say as I put the car in park. I think of a million different ways I could take that dress off. Instead, I take her hand in mine and gently kiss it.

She blushes and turns away momentarily. When her eyes meet mine again, I notice that her cheeks are pink. That's something else that I remember about her.

"Thank you." She smiles. "I'm just glad Emma was able to grab it for me." A look of disappointment crosses her face, and her shoulders tense up.

"Grab it for you?" I ask. I kiss her hand again and try to ignore the diamond ring on her finger. I can't. It pisses me off that I can't.

She nods. "Colton, my ex. He hasn't been so cooperative, and…"

"Hey," I whisper. "You don't have to explain." *But please explain,* I think. *Did you love him? Do you love him?* Obviously, if she was going to marry Colton, she loved him at least enough to say yes to a proposal.

"No, it's okay," she says. "It's just that I haven't had much access to my closet. I think he's holding my shoes hostage, actually." She presses her lips together in a slight pout. "He isn't very happy with me," she adds. Cassidy shrugs and glances down at the diamond.

But you still wear his ring, I think.

Her eyes meet mine, and I think she reads my mind. They are sorrowful and weary, but man, they are pretty. The green in her dress makes her eyes pop, and I'm trying to listen, but it is so hard to focus. She unbuckles her seat belt and leans toward me, wrapping her arm around mine, then rests her head on my shoulder. I hear the steady sound of her breathing, and she is quiet for a beat. She twirls a strand of hair around her finger and nuzzles further into my neck. "I'm kind of an asshole," she says.

I laugh and cup her cheek with my hand. "You are the least assholish person I know."

"I don't think that's a word." She chuckles. "But you are the writer, not me."

I squeeze her tight, impressed that she remembers how much I love writing.

We are quiet for a minute before she closes her eyes and blurts, "I left him. At the altar."

"Your fiancé? Like, on your wedding day?" I know my words aren't gentle, but holy shit, that takes guts. It's worse than I first thought. She was really getting married. Like, ready to have the wedding, guests invited, money spent. My mind whirls, and I try to keep a straight face, but I can tell by her reaction that I am doing a terrible job.

"See? I'm an asshole."

I'm quiet for a moment as I study her face. She doesn't seem sad about the breakup. Honestly, I could care less about the dude she left at the altar; I am just relieved that she didn't marry him. I'm glad that I made it in time. I guess sometimes you have to realize what you have lost before you can appreciate it. It sounds like maybe that is what happened with her too. *So take the stupid ring off, Cass.*

She starts to open the car door. "We should get inside."

"Hey," I say.

She pauses and turns to meet my gaze. I need the right words. How do I tell her how I'm feeling? How do I tell her that I don't give a shit about whatever loser she was engaged to? How do I explain to this person that I have very recently come to realize she just might be the woman of my dreams?

"I marked you down for the steak. For dinner," I exclaim. "I hope that's okay."

* * *

I WAS RIGHT ABOUT high school reunions: they really aren't for me. I don't know who half of these people are, but the ironic part is that they remember me. For the first time in my life, I am thankful for name tags.

I am also grateful for the spunky little redhead who stands next to me during cocktails with her arm wrapped around mine, smiling and nodding as if she gives a rat's ass about Maggie and her promotion from assistant principal to actual principal or Mark and his overachieving twin girls. She sips her wine and says things like, "It is so great that you take the time to coach softball. It is something they will never forget," and "That is so exciting! See? Hard work pays off!" I knew she would be a good plus-one. I'm relieved that nobody has asked anything about our relationship.

When we finally have a moment alone, we are outside the Union Bluff Hotel, standing on the grass that overlooks the shore of Short Sands Beach. The tide is out, and the sand seems to extend for miles, and I can't really tell where the water meets land. The sky is clear with the exception of a few pink-and-yellow wispy clouds that seem to shimmer as they reflect off the water.

"It's stunning," Cassidy whispers. She is standing in front of me, and my arms are draped around her shoulders. She sips her wine with one hand and places the other behind my head, turning slowly to face me.

"*You're* stunning," I say.

She leans forward and kisses me. I feel like fifteen years have been erased, and we are twentysomething again. I'm intoxicated by her kiss more than from the wine. I had forgotten how powerful my feelings are for this woman. I kiss her back and pull her close, feeling an overwhelming sense of gratitude for second chances.

* * *

WE ALMOST OPT out of dinner, but Cassidy claims it wouldn't be considered actually attending the reunion if we don't stay for the meal. We are seated at a table with four other couples that I don't recognize or have any remembrance of, but apparently Jason and I had sophomore drivers' ed together, and Joanne and I shared similar classes all four years. Jason has three kids and is married to a tall brunette named Melissa. Joanne is now a published writer and has come to the reunion with a friend, as she has recently divorced.

Joanne takes every opportunity to poke at my writing career and seems very eager to know what I have been up to. If I didn't know any better, I would think that she was also a bit interested in getting into my pants.

"Most of my work has been self-published, but I am working on getting an agent for a new series I'm writing," she brags. "How about you, Sean? I remember your short stories being captivating."

As she says this, she leans forward. I awkwardly look away so I'm not staring down her dress. Her lipstick is hot pink and makes her mouth look huge and overwhelming. I have a mouthful of steak, so I chew slowly to buy myself some time to think.

"Thank you," I finally manage and take a sip of my drink. "I'm glad you like my stuff from high school, because I sure can't remember a damn thing I wrote. It was *so* long ago." I tap my mouth with my linen napkin and carefully place it on my lap as Cass takes my hand in hers and chuckles.

Joanne straightens and studies my expression as if she is trying to figure out if I'm serious or not. "So you aren't writing anymore then?" she pries. Joanne's date is very focused on eating his dinner and barely looks up. Joanne smiles. "It's okay if you aren't. Writer's block is a real thing."

I feel my cheeks get red, and I take a sip of my drink. Tiny beads of sweat are making their way down the crease of my back, and I suddenly need to take off this damn jacket and get outside. Of course I wanted to be published by now. And yeah, I crushed high school creative writing, but none of that matters now. And of course I remember my short stories.

The table is silent for a beat, and Cass places her hand on my knee, jolting me back to the present. "Oh, he has been writing," she says in a very matter-of-fact tone.

I stare at her in confusion, and her eyes go wide. Her hand squeezes my knee. I decide to play along, if for no other reason than to shut up the pink-lipped freak across the table. Cass rubs her hand along my leg, and my anxiety calms, but the rest of me is suddenly focused on one thing: her hand on my thigh.

"Sean has been writing for years. He has tons of stuff." She rolls her eyes and motions with her hand as if to say "Totally not a big deal." "Besides," she continues, confidently and eagerly. She holds up her left hand and shrieks in a tone I have never heard her use, but only I could know is fake. "We are getting married! Sean has been way too busy helping me with our plans to be stuck in front of a computer." She grins.

The company at our table oohs and aahs over Cassidy's ring.

"How could I not know that?" someone asks. "Oh yeah, you are like invisible on social."

Joanne excuses herself from the table, and I squeeze Cassidy's knee with my sweaty palm. Her short dress leaves her legs bare, and her skin is soft and smooth beneath my fingers.

Cassidy has her cell phone out and is typing. She kisses the side of my chin as if we have been together for years and leans in to whisper in my ear. "Read your texts."

I nonchalantly reach into my jacket and pull out my cell. I have a few missed texts from people back home, but I click on Cassidy's name.

Cass: I am ready to get the hell out of here if you are.

I try my best to hide my smile and type my reply.

Sean: Are you sure? I am having so much fun. NOT. Don't you want dessert?

I SMILE AGAIN, bigger this time, and watch her type her reply. She is biting her lower lip. Her mouth curves into a playful grin. I wonder what she is typing.

"When is the wedding?" someone at our table asks.

Cassidy is texting but doesn't miss a beat. "Oh, we haven't set a date yet. But we are thinking next summer. Right on Long Sands." She smiles, winking at me. She continues, "Where we first met."

I laugh and squeeze her knee. My phone vibrates on my lap.

Cass: Let's get out of here. I'll be your dessert ;)

NOW- CASSIDY

CHAPTER FOURTEEN

*I*t is a heated ride home, but now, on my couch, I am finally pulling off his sport coat and unbuttoning his shirt. He smells amazing. He feels unbelievable. His cheek presses against mine, so soft and familiar. His lips kiss my face and meet my lips. His hands rub through the back of my hair, and he squeezes me close to him. My legs are wrapped around his waist, and he kisses me harder and holds me tighter. I can't resist opening my eyes so I can see him.

His eyes are closed, his expression intense. I notice that this moment looks way more emotional for him than I realized. I can sense it in his movements, in his breathing. He is falling as hard and fast as I am, and at this moment, I realize that this night is not going to end with us sleeping together, and I am almost relieved.

I pull back slowly and study his expression. We are both sweating, our hearts beating fast, and I can't tell which one of us is shaking.

"Are you okay?" I ask, flooding his forehead with kisses.

"Cass," he breathes heavily, "you make me so happy."

I nod and kiss the tip of his nose. "Mhmmm," I moan. "Same."

He stops kissing me and cups my face with his hands. "I know this is crazy. I know it's nuts to feel this way."

"Why?" I ask. Then I realize that I know just what he means. I know this because his fingers are now playing with the engagement ring on my left hand.

"We can't," he says. "Not like this."

I nod in agreement. "I know, and I'm sorry." I shake my head. "I don't love Colton, not like...I mean, I was..."

Not like I love you, I want to say. Being with Colton didn't even compare to the way I feel being with Sean. Does that even make sense? We haven't talked in fifteen years! But it's there, and I feel it. I cringe in aggravation, partly because I can't find the right words but also because I am frustrated. Is it okay to allow the concept of time to put an emotional cap on something that was so real—*is* real?

"Not like what?" he asks. I can tell that he is resentful with himself for stopping this, for stopping us. But it is the right thing to do.

I release his hands and place them around my waist, pulling him close to me. "Listen," I say, rather surprised by the boldness of my tone. "I get it." I kiss the spot on the side of his earlobe that I know he can't resist.

"Seriously, Cassidy?" he begs in a frustrated whisper. I am overly ecstatic that after all this time, his body still responds this way.

"We don't have to sleep together tonight, but I also can't let you leave."

He squeezes me tighter and reciprocates my kisses and muffles some comments about my green dress and my legs, but I'm not really able to understand. I hadn't planned on my dress being so short, but by the time Emma showed up with it this afternoon, I had no other option. I was a little worried that I looked slutty, but I fit right in at Sean's reunion.

And it is coming in handy. Sean has shimmied my dress up to my waist so that it fits more like a shirt then a dress anyhow. His eager hands have secured themselves tightly around my hips. My mind is racing, and I try hard to stop thinking, but I'm not ready to lose control. My mind skips back to our last time being this intimate, our last night together in his room before our summer ended. Sean and I did not sleep together that night. We were the perfect after-school special on "everything but," as Emma liked to call it, but we stopped before actually sleeping together.

I have wondered many times over the years what it would have been like. I've pictured us together, having that perfect moment. And in this familiar juncture with Sean, I am desperate to go further. But we don't have to, and in some twisted way, this kind of makes me love him more.

He traces his fingernails from my lower back to my thighs, and I gasp out loud when I realize he has not lost his touch. His mouth finds my neck and moves to my chest, and I am no longer consciously thinking about anything other than Sean. Sean's body, Sean's heart, Sean's...extremities. My body responds to him even more than it did years ago. My eyes, facial expressions, and words all have minds of their own. My brain is somewhere else. I am out of my body, watching us rock together on the new black sofa, the leather sticking on the parts of me that are no longer dressed.

When we come back to Earth, I realize that we have somehow ended up intertwined on the floor. I stand up quickly, eager to pull my clothes back on and start fixing my dress. I am suddenly surprised that I feel somewhat awkward about the state of my hair, my makeup, and, well, everything. The fact that I have been lying here with Sean should make me feel at ease, but instead, I am regretting how vulnerable I just allowed myself to be.

"Cass," he says again. "I need you to take it off."

"My dress?" I ask awkwardly.

"No." He laughs, pulling my hands toward him. "The ring," he pleads.

"Oh." I chuckle in embarrassment. "I thought you meant..." My voice trails off yet again, and he shakes his head, the side of his lip curling up, his eyes not leaving mine.

"The ring," he whispers.

"The ring," I repeat. I don't know what to say, so I kiss the top of his nose then his mouth then his chest. I'm not sure what I can say about Colton's ring at this moment, but for now, I will kiss Sean a lot and hope that this works.

"Cass," he whispers.

I nod as if agreeing with him and place my finger over his lips. "Come to bed?" I ask hopefully.

"You were always really good about changing the subject."

I take his hand in mine, leading him to my bedroom.

* * *

HE STAYS with me all night. I believe spooning is what the kids are calling it these days. My back and my bottom are pressed firmly into his core, and his arms don't let me go. I've always said I'm not much of a cuddler, but in this case, it is different. I don't want him to let me go.

I have no immediate plans to remove my engagement ring. I don't understand why, but I know that both Sean and Colton deserve better than that. I know my engagement is over. And I truly understand that Colton is not the one for me. This still makes me sad and a bit regretful.

Colton might not have been the love of my life, but he was good to me. I think that is why I feel so guilty and why I won't take the ring off. But how do I explain that to this man who has been gone from my life for fifteen freaking years and is calling me the woman of his dreams? What if this is a huge life rebound for both of us? A huge mistake?

My body awakens and tells my mind to quiet down, because Sean is awake and is kissing the back of my neck.

"Good morning," I whisper.

"This…" he states between kisses, "this…is…most definitely a good morning."

His arms scoop under mine, and his shirtless chest presses against the back of me. He is warm against me, and I am melting. My mind stops its downward spiral, and I sigh. Reaching behind me, I grab his legs and wrap them around my body.

"You make me crazy." I chuckle.

"You're already crazy."

I wiggle out of his embrace and turn so I am facing him. Last night, he was so clean-cut with his fresh shave, and this morning, bits of scruff appear in all the right places. He has bed head, and I am immediately overcome with joy that we are together in this moment. I never in a million years would have ever thought this to be a possibility again.

"What's so funny?"

"You."

My mouth covers his, and his whiskers scrape my bottom lip. He kisses my neck and my chest, something he has done before, but it still feels new. My hands take on a mind of their own and are grabbing at him and feeling him, exploring his naked chest, his waist, his back, his arms. My senses are on overload. I can smell the remains of the cologne he used last night for the reunion and the salt air from the open window next to us. I can taste the toothpaste he borrowed from me last night. I hope more than anything that he will need to borrow it again tonight.

* * *

Diary of Cassidy Quinn
>   Day #50
>   Dear Diary,
>   I am in love. That's all.

Day #55

I found my #15. Sean Anderson. Makes me happy. He makes ALL of me happy. When Emma asked if we were sleeping together yet and I told her no, she criticized me to no end. When I explained to her just how many times (5 times in a row) Sean was able to make me "happy," as we called it in high school, she told me to marry him.

Speaking of getting married, Colton's mother called me this morning. Sean heard the whole conversation while we were still in bed. She said I need to go pick up my things. She hired someone to pack them up, but I need to come get them. She was organizing this because Colton doesn't want to see me. I don't really blame him. And he wants his ring back.

I arranged with Emma to meet me in the city next week, but Sean was insisting on coming to help. I told him it would be too awkward and assured him that Emma and I could handle it. I had been so angry with Colton's mother that I actually took the diamond off my finger and chucked it across the room. Sean laughed and pulled me on top of him. Asked me if I was ready to go for number six.

NOW- SEAN

CHAPTER FIFTEEN

Stephanie: (5 days ago) Are you around?
Stephanie: (5 days ago) Want to hook up later?
Stephanie: (3 days ago) Sean?
Stephanie: (3 days ago) You haven't been to the gym lately. I was wondering if you are okay?
Stephanie: (1 day ago) Sean?
Stephanie: (44 minutes ago) ?
Stephanie: (42 minutes ago) I was thinking maybe your kitchen counter missed me? I'll bring beers. What do you say? (Insert topless photo)
Stephanie: (2 minutes ago) I can take a hint. Lose my number.

Josie: (7 days ago) Hey babe are you back in Cali?
Josie: (5 days ago) IMU
Josie: (1 day ago) Went to your place. Brought your mail in.
Josie: (20 minutes ago) Sean? I'm worried

Chad: (3 days ago) Yo bro, rad barrels out there! Wanna join?

Chad: (1 day ago) Hey! You out gettin laid again? You missed some killer waves.

Chad: (20 minutes ago) You dead mon?

I toss my phone onto the couch next to me and snicker at Chad's *Cool Runnings* reference. Clearly my peeps back in Cali aren't too happy with me, especially Stephanie. The truth is I'm a little embarrassed about some of it. Being back home has reminded me so much of Grandpa, and the way I was living back west would be really disappointing to him. And now that I have Cass back, the thought of being with some of these other women basically makes my skin crawl.

I quickly delete the naked photo from my phone. I've been around the block enough to appreciate how much trouble that could get me into with my girlfriend.

Girlfriend. I love the sound of it. We were out for drinks last night at the piano bar, and I lost a bet with her about the year the bar was established and ended up belting out an interesting classical-sounding version of "Livin' on a Prayer." After a solid standing ovation by all (well, most) of the intoxicated tourists in the house, I invited my girlfriend Cassidy up to join me for my next song. If looks could kill, I would have been dead instantly, but I think I survived because I called her my girlfriend. We belted out our own unique version of "Sweet Caroline" and had the place jumping. Afterward, we walked home, hand in hand, a little tipsy from our mojitos.

"I really like that bar," I said as we crossed the street onto Seaberry Lane, the air from the sea just cool enough.

"I really like being your girlfriend," she replied matter-of-factly and squeezed my hand tighter.

I chuckled and sighed with relief as I wrapped my hand around hers and didn't feel a diamond.

THAT WAS LAST NIGHT, and now today, she and Emma are on their mission to pick up Cassidy's things from Colton. I pick up my cell phone again, and in an effort to ignore everyone I'm ghosting, I check out my last text from Cassidy.

CASSIDY: Emma and I got my things. We will be back by dinner. You sure you don't mind if I use storage?

I type quickly, noticing that it is only two o'clock and feeling instantly disappointed that she isn't closer to home. She will drop some stuff off in storage and bring other things up this way. Feels good to know she isn't setting up camp back in Boston. The idea of her needing storage in York is settling somehow. Like, she might not be leaving too soon, perhaps?

Sean: Bring as much back as you need. We will find room. Grandpa also has an attic and nobody goes up there so if you need more space it's yours.
Cassidy: TY
Sean: Did it go ok?
Cassidy: About as good as it could have. See you soon

* * *

THE REST of the afternoon goes slowly. I head into town and get a cup of coffee at a place where Grandpa and I would have breakfast every weekend before he was sick. I observe the tourists and people watch for a bit before heading over to the Nubble Lighthouse. I park where Cassidy and I used to make out and marvel at how it has not changed a bit, not in fifteen years and not since I climbed on these rocks as a kid. Grandpa warned me not to slip as I bounced from stone to stone. He loved it there as much as I did.

I spend the remainder of the afternoon organizing Grandpa's attic, a place I haven't stepped foot in for who knows how long. After Grandpa passed, I left for California and didn't look back—until now. Joey was in charge of packing up everything for me. Most things went into the basement. The attic wasn't huge, but it was enough.

My back aches from not being able to stand up straight, and a thick fog of dust kicks up around me as I shove boxes to the perimeter in an effort to give Cass room for her things. Most of the boxes are labeled *cottage* or *Anderson*, but tucked away in the corner under plastic sheeting is a green trunk that I don't recognize. I wonder if Joey has borrowed some of this space for his own personal use and almost head back down the ladder. It is getting late, and I need to shower before dinner. But instead, an interesting spark of curiosity —inspiration?— hits me in a way it hasn't in years.

I crawl over to the trunk, careful not to hit my head or land my knees on any of the nails that are sticking up around me. I decide I don't like small spaces and almost bail again, but the piece of masking tape over the top of the trunk reads "Gerry's things," and I realize that I would give anything to have a piece of Grandpa that is new—at least to me—even if it means suffering through this dust bath. I pull it across the attic with all the strength I can muster and ease it down the ladder.

A strange sense of anticipation flows through my veins, and I am suddenly eager to crack this puppy open. I drag it into the living room and prop the screen door open, thankful for the relief of the fresh air.

I begin digging through the trunk and find photo after photo, all black and white, in various sizes. There's one of my grandmother, Rosemary, propped up on the rocks by the Nubble Lighthouse, and another of her on a horse. There's a three-by-five of her holding a baby (I'm assuming my father) right in the same spot Cassidy and I walked hand in hand last night. I also find photographs of Grandpa with my father as a boy; a portrait of him in a Navy uniform, saluting with pride; a painting of the Nubble Lighthouse signed with my grandmother's initials, RA.

I remember how much he talked about Grandma. They met when he was in France. I don't remember the details about when or how they met, but I do know that he loved her very much. He was lost after she passed away. I must have been four years old or five maybe. She died from a complication with her heart and, soon afterward, a stroke.

Sometimes I can't fathom how my mom and dad could just move out west and forget about their lives here. I'm sure they had their reasons. And didn't I do the same thing? I tell myself that my moving away was different, that I didn't leave a family behind, all the while knowing now that I did—because I left Cassidy, and now more than ever, I realize that she is my family. I will never leave her again.

I dig deeper in the trunk and discover a strongbox I've never seen. A couple of medals fall out, and I realize they are Grandpa's medals from the time he served in the Navy. I knew he had earned a Purple Heart, but I've never seen it before.

I find more medals, some postcards, and a collection of drink stirrers from various restaurants. A drink stirrer from the piano bar in town makes me chuckle.

And then there is a ring of keys. I toss them to the side and continue digging, suddenly more inspired than ever, feeling like a pirate who has found his treasure or a detective uncovering a cold case or, even better, a guy with writer's block getting ideas for a story.

I glance at the clock and tell myself it's time to stop, but I can't. I keep digging. I come across Grandpa's bowling shoes and another strongbox that opens easily, revealing three different mismatched earrings, one brass key, and one jeweler's box. I open it and realize that it holds an engagement ring I have never seen before. The gold is a bit tarnished, but the diamond is still flawless, almost shiny. A part of me wonders how much money I could get for it, but the other part of me sets it down safely next to the key. My search continues, and I discover Grandpa's bowling ball and a pair of faded pink baby booties.

And here's another locked box. Taking a chance, I grab the key, and sure enough, the box pops open. Another round of dust nails me in my face. I sneeze and continue looking through the box. Black-and-white photos as well as letters, a stack of envelopes, and a collection of coins fill this box.

I decide that my search has probably gone on long enough for the night and begin to put everything back. Cassidy will be pulling in soon and will need help unloading the U-Haul. I promise myself I will continue my search tomorrow, as the inspiration running through me is endless.

I curse under my breath when my elbow knocks over my beer and move quickly to remove any of my new treasures from its reach. I scurry over to the paper towels and wipe it up.

A few of the pictures have fallen from the locked box. I laugh to myself as I see one of a younger version of Joey—way younger, probably not even in his twenties. He's a handsome guy, strong looking with a proud smile, standing right in front of the Nubble. I flip to the next and see a very young version of Grandpa as well, standing in the same spot, holding hands with a woman I haven't seen before. It doesn't even take until the count of three before I am blown away by the familiarity of her smile and those eyes.

I flip the photo over and read Grandpa's chicken scratch. I'm so startled by what I read that I can hardly turn it back over fast enough to reexamine the woman in the photo.

"Holy shit," I say aloud.

I hear the storm door open and shut behind me and realize it is Cassidy.

"Hey there! I missed you," she exclaims and approaches me for a quick embrace. "Are you okay? You are filthy! What is all of this?" She laughs.

I try to find the words, but I can't seem to put them together. Instead, I hand her the photograph and let her see for herself. She flips the photo over and reads the caption aloud. "Eyes as green as the sea...My Dolly (1939)." Her eyes widen, and she flips it back over and quickly scans the image.

"What the hell?" I'm finally able to ask.

She looks at the photo, then at me, and then back at the photograph. "Where did you get this?"

"In the attic."

"This attic?"

"Yes. Cass, who is that?"

"It's a photo of my Grandmother, Gwendoline. I just don't understand why you have it."

"Your grandmother? Cassidy, the guy in the photo is Grandpa."

"My grandmother with your grandfather," she affirms. "What in the hell is going on?"

PART FOUR

SPRING OF 1942

CHAPTER SIXTEEN

"*W*hat are you thinking about?" His question seemed innocent enough, but considering the circumstances, it was not. I settled my head on his shoulder and sighed. It was a beautiful day, but I just couldn't enjoy it. I typically found comfort in the rhythmic pattern of the waves as they crashed and disintegrated against the rocks. But not today. Today, I couldn't find much joy in anything.

We were in the front seat of his father's Cadillac, parked overlooking the Nubble Lighthouse. He had just polished the car, and the glare from the sun was starting to hurt my head. That, along with everything else that was happening, was enough to make me want to press my foot firmly on the gas pedal myself and drive us straight off the cliff and into the dark ocean water.

"It's going to be okay," he whispered into my ear.

His voice was calm, but I wasn't buying it. I could tell he was saying these things to me so that I would calm down, and I was growing tired of that.

"You can't promise me that you will come back in one piece," I said firmly, pulling away and looking outside, adjusting my beret. "Gerald Thomas Anderson, you just can't make that promise." I bit my lower lip in an effort to keep the tears inside. I released my hand from his and pulled my skirt tight around my legs.

"Gwendoline," he began.

"You never call me Gwendoline," I spat.

"Dolly." He smirked. I squeezed his arm around mine. "It's all going to be okay. I would rather enlist now than get drafted later."

"Well, that's good then," I huffed. "At least you aren't digging your own grave against your will." I crossed my arms over my chest.

"Don't be angry," he begged.

"I'm not angry with you."

I turned toward him and wrapped my arms around his shoulders, burying my face in his neck. My tears left marks on his white collared shirt. I wasn't angry with him, but I had had enough of this war. I had been listening to the radio with my father when we got word of what happened at Pearl Harbor. I knew in my heart that once Gerry heard the news, he would want to be first on the list to go and help. Sure enough, less than a week after the attack, he had made his decision.

"I'm proud of you. Everything is just so crummy," I admitted.

And I was scared of losing him. I had spent the past year already worried about the thought of my own father and brother being drafted. I figured that if I was to lose any of them to this battle, it would be because they had no other choice.

"Do you think we can try and be strong?" he asked.

I nodded in agreement. One of the things I loved about him was his desire to make a difference. How could I blame him for accepting the opportunity to help? Most of my teenage life had focused on the war. Sitting and listening to the radio with my father had become a tradition I'd started to look forward to. We sat together, eating sardines and crackers, sometimes bored and sometimes shocked with the news of an invasion or attack. My heart would break as I learned of the sacrifices soldiers were making for their countries. If I had been a man, I would probably have enlisted myself.

"I can...I mean, I will," I agree. "Just promise me, Gerry. Promise me you will stay safe. Pray that you will come home to me."

"I'm praying harder than you know, Dolly," he said. "Now go on. Dry your eyes. Everything will be okay."

* * *

AN HOUR LATER, we were climbing the steps to his cottage. The large gray house seemed to tower over the others on Long Sands Beach. His parents lived on the second floor, where Gerry had lived until recently. After years of begging and persuading, he had been granted permission to stay on the first floor by himself, which was really quite the big deal. The home had been in their family for generations, and the first floor had been reserved for tenants and extended family only. Since Gerry had recently turned eighteen, Mr. and Mrs. Anderson had decided to give him the living space. I had wondered to myself if it was a last attempt on their part to keep him from enlisting in the Navy.

I, of course, still lived with my parents in our small cottage across town. Being the only child and still at the young age of seventeen, I was strongly forbidden to be alone with Gerry on that first floor. When my father spoke of his living situation, it almost sounded as though he was comparing the first floor of that house to the bowels of hell.

He actually threatened to shoot Gerry with his shotgun if he got word of us disobeying.

THE COTTAGE WAS warm and inviting anytime I entered it. On this particular evening, Gerry's father, George Anderson, was settled in his brown-and-black-plaid armchair, cigar in hand. Mrs. Anderson was busy in the kitchen, preparing the roast for dinner. I hugged and kissed her hello and handed her a cherry nut cake my mother had baked that morning. Gerry lit a cigar of his own and sat on the sofa near his father.

"Gwendoline," his mom called from the stove, "would you be a love and set the table?"

"Of course, Mrs. Anderson," I replied.

"You boys better be washed up and ready for dinner in thirty minutes," she called to Gerry and Mr. Anderson. "I invited the Chase family from upstairs to come down for dinner in celebration of Gerry's news."

Gerry's news? How was this a celebration?

"Yes, ma'am," Gerry replied.

"And Gerry?"

"Momma?"

"You fell asleep last night in your father's chair again with that cigar in your mouth. One of these days, you are going to wake up in a pile of ashes if you aren't careful."

* * *

MY STOMACH WAS full from dinner, but my heart was still feeling empty. The car seemed quieter than normal as Gerry drove me back home. I knew these roads like the back of my hand. Without the ocean breeze, I felt suffocated. The beauty that encompassed me here was really all I needed. That and my Gerry.

Just because I was only seventeen didn't mean I didn't know what true love was. Gerry had asked me on my first date when I was only fourteen years old. He took me for pizza, and we went bowling. We strolled along Short Sands Beach for hours. I didn't feel like the fourteen-year-old girl I was. When he held my hand in the moonlight and softly kissed my forehead, I felt like the queen of the world. I clearly remembered thinking to myself that I could marry Gerald Anderson, this boy from Long Sands Beach.

As if reading my mind, he pulled over to the side of the road overlooking Long Sands. The shore was secluded, and I marveled at the stretch of wet sand extending toward the horizon. The stillness of the water during low tide never ceased to take my breath away. The ripples that formed on the hard, wet sand made it almost impossible to tell where the water met land.

"It's low tide!" I exclaimed.

"Yes, ma'am."

"Could we go just for a little while?"

"Of course," he answered, kissing my forehead softly.

I rested my forehead against his and, for a brief second, was at ease.

The tide being out so far made it easy to pull up my polka-dotted dress and skip through the water. "I don't see any sea glass," he admitted. "But I do see lots of shells."

"You have to look harder," I called back, swishing and swirling through the ankle-deep water. My red curls bounced over my shoulders and hit my eyes as I spun. The coldness of the water pierced my ankles like needles but felt intoxicating. "It's like looking for treasure!"

He laughed and ran toward me, trudging through the water with ease. He scooped me up from behind and twirled me around. "I don't need any more treasure," he whispered. "I already found mine." Gerry kissed my cheeks and then my lips and my cheeks again.

"I love you, Gerry Anderson," I said.

"Wait!" he shouted.

"What?" I asked, jumping back in alarm. "What is it?"

"I found something!"

"Oh, any sea glass?"

"Nope," he said, dropping to one knee.

"Gerry, you are getting soaked!" I squealed. "Get out of that water. Your mother is going to throw a fit, you knucklehead."

At that moment, I stopped in midsentence as I realized Gerry was down on one knee, and stretched out in front of me was a small black-velvet box. My heart actually stopped beating for a moment, and the ground seemed to move beneath me.

"Gwendoline Ellis...Dolly...I love you more than life itself."

"Oh, Gerry!" I covered my face with my hands. Unable to control my emotions, I allowed my ankle-length dress to float lightly over each rush of water. Gerry...my Gerry in the ocean on one knee.

"Would you make me the happiest man alive and marry me?"

"Yes!" I shouted at the top of my lungs. "Yes, Gerry, I will marry you!"

"Hot diggity dog!" he cheered as he placed the ring on my finger.

He picked me up, twirled me around, and tripped. We both fell into the water, me on top of him. We rolled around in those waves for what seemed like hours. The coldness of the water disappeared altogether as we kissed, cried, hoped, and prayed that maybe we would actually make it through this. Maybe there was a light at the end of the tunnel after all.

* * *

THAT NIGHT WAS the best night of my life. I would never forget how ridiculous we both must have looked. But then again, I suppose that love might look ridiculous sometimes. His white collared shirt had stuck to his body, probably ruined by the saltwater, but neither of us cared. My hair was matted to my forehead, and my makeup ran down my face. My dress was completely and utterly drenched. When I got home, my mother said I looked like a drowned rat and began to scold me, but her tone quickly changed when I showed her my engagement ring. She was thrilled for us, and my father was as well.

We were married on July 1, 1942 in front of the Union Bluff Hotel, overlooking Short Sands Beach, in a very small ceremony that included my family, his family, and Joey Chase, Gerry's best friend. It was an absolutely perfect day, even more perfect than I'd ever imagined it could be. The sun shined bright, and the waves were calm. Tourists and spectators splashed in the waves as they looked on. I stood elegantly in the white dress my mother had made, hand in hand with the love of my life.

"I will love you forever and always, Gwendoline Ellis— Dolly." He was exceptionally handsome in his formal Navy uniform.

"I will love you forever and always, no matter what, Gerald Anderson."

We kissed the longest kiss, longer than my father probably cared for. But the spectators watching from the water cheered, hooted, and whistled.

* * *

I PRAYED over and over again that he would change his mind. Maybe he might realize that we could be starting our lives together. Although I knew he was doing the right thing and serving his country, a piece of me thought, *Couldn't someone else go? Why Gerry?*

I had been very unsettled since the draft started anyhow. My brother hadn't been drafted after all because he had flat feet. I told Gerry he should lie and say his feet were flat. He laughed and told me someone would notice they weren't. I told him we could run away to Canada and start our own lives, just him and me.

"Only a chicken runs away," he had said. "I love my country too much for that. And anyway, I'm no coward."

"Do you love your country more than you love me?" I asked.

He told me that wasn't fair and not to worry so much. He would return to me in one piece.

We spent the rest of our summer together on the beach. By August, we were renting the first floor of the cottage. I found joy in taking care of my husband in the little time we had together. He worked during the day, and I took care of our cozy piece of heaven.

Even though we had our own floor of the cottage, it was still hard to be alone. One of our parents seemed to always be popping in. We spent our nights on the rocks by the lighthouse. We walked Short Sands and Long Sands. We parked at Short Sands and Long Sands. Usually when we parked, we just talked and kissed, but as his date of departure grew closer and my nerves worsened, sometimes we fought in his car. And sometimes after an argument, we ended up in the back seat, making love. So great was our passion that one night, the windows were so steamy we needed to roll them down and drive home very slowly to air them out.

I loved being Mrs. Anderson and waking up next to my husband each morning. He mesmerized me in every way. I considered each moment that we spent together a gift, a blessing. The nights we went dancing were my favorite. Sometimes we went alone, just the two of us, and other times, Joey Chase and his friends would join. Gerry didn't love to dance, but he never turned down a slow song. He often sent me off with Joey Chase—Joey had to buy my husband a beer for every dance we had. Gerry always enjoyed our version of the jitterbug and even the Lindy Hop jive that we had perfected over the years.

Everything felt perfect, and I started to feel hopeful that we might be able to beat the odds and overcome these times. But sure enough, on September 1, 1942, Gerry boarded a train for Newport, Rhode Island, where he would spend thirteen weeks in training before heading overseas.

We wrote letters to each other constantly, and he poured his heart out to me more than I ever expected. He talked about things he was learning to do, people he met, and most importantly, all of the incredible things we would do upon his return. In one of his last letters from training, he told me that he didn't know where they were sending him, but it would be a European country. He would keep me updated and promised me he would stay safe.

When he went overseas, it was the worst day of my life. My heart swapped quickly from angry to sad and back again. I spent night after night at the Nubble alone, pretending that he was there with me and fooling myself with words that should have been spoken to him but instead were left to the stars.

I wrote to him, one letter for each day that he was gone. Each day, I wanted to hear from him. I needed to hear from him. Lots of my acquaintances were in the same boat as me. Many of them had sent husbands, brothers, uncles, and fathers overseas. Some chose war, but for others, war chose them.

But not all of them. Joey Chase had not been drafted. Luck of the draw? An answer to his mother's prayer? I was relieved for him but wondered why my luck couldn't have been the same. Why did my husband choose to go?

Joey had attended the Anderson family dinners often since Gerry's departure. He brought with him a sense of comfort and humor, telling us funny stories about him and Gerry as kids. It brought smiles to the faces of Mr. and Mrs. Anderson, but not to mine. I grew resentful at times as I watched him with the Andersons, fighting off jealous thoughts for Gerry as I watched Mr. Anderson and Joey sharing cigars in the living room or how Mrs. Anderson laughed at Joey's jokes like she used to laugh with Gerry.

I lay awake night after night, yelling and crying. One night, I was crying so loudly that Mrs. Anderson heard me from upstairs and came down, nightgown and all. She crawled into bed and held me, comforting me like a child.

"I miss him," I wailed, shoving my fist into the down pillow. Feathers exploded upward and stuck to my tear-streaked cheeks.

"I miss him too," she whispered time and time again, holding me until I was asleep.

AND THAT WAS how it was. Day after day, I received no word from Gerry. No letters, no postcards, no information. Some of my friends with boyfriends or husbands at war would get written communication of some kind, but not us. Not from Gerry. One Saturday morning, I went up to the third floor of the cottage to see if Joey Chase had heard from him. He said that he hadn't received anything either but not to worry.

After a month of being without him, I became withdrawn. My nightmares grew worse. I didn't want to go outside, even to the ocean. Why would I want to stand there and stare out at the water and the edge of the earth? Somewhere out there, Gerry was on some ship, shooting at people or even getting shot at—or even worse, dead at sea, floating belly up, only to be left as food for the sharks. What was the point?

Soon after that, I stopped eating altogether. I cried all day and all night. My mother came over to check on me, and I could hear her telling Mrs. Anderson that it was time for me to come home, that I was just a child and this wasn't healthy. Mrs. Anderson was in rare form too, worried about her son.

My mother suggested getting a job like most of the Navy wives were doing. She encouraged me to get out and be with them. My father offered to drive me to the factory with him, where many of my friends took shifts to pass the time or make ends meet. The truth was that I had lost touch with most of my girlfriends when I started seeing Gerry. He was my world.

Mrs. Anderson told my mother that I would be okay, and we would surely be hearing from him soon. No news was good news after all.

WINTER OF 1942- GWENDOLINE

CHAPTER SEVENTEEN

I heard the knock at the door, but I refused to answer. It was surely going to be the war department with a telegram notifying me of Gerry's death. I knew this because he had to be dead.

"Gwen, open up. It's me, Joey."

I jumped up from my bed and wrapped a blanket around my shoulders. I let him in, and he was followed by a wave of cold air.

"Have you heard from him?" I begged.

"No," he sighed. "Nothing yet."

"I just don't understand. I'm writing to him every day. Where are my letters going?"

Joey shook his head in discouragement and shrugged. "Don't flip your wig, Gwendoline. Nobody has heard from him."

I took his coat and hat and hung them up on the hook by the door, as I had done almost daily for the past couple weeks or so. He thanked me and walked toward the kitchenette. He put the kettle on the stove and began boiling water for tea.

I sat on the couch and wrapped the blanket around me tightly. Strands of red wisped out of my bun, and I fiddled with my hairpin.

"Did you eat today?" he asked.

I shook my head and looked away. I tried to come up with some excuse, but he interrupted me.

"Gwendoline, you need to eat. It isn't going to do Gerry any good when he comes home to find you starved to death."

I knew he was right, but did he really need to be so crass? Where did he get off telling me what to do? I was certainly not a child. But I knew he was right. It just didn't feel okay to eat when Gerry might be dead.

Moments later, Joey returned from the kitchen with toast and margarine and a cup of tea.

"Thank you."

"You're welcome."

"You don't have to do this every day," I mumbled between bites.

"I know."

"Why *do* you then?" The tea tasted perfect and warmed my body from my lips to my toes.

"Maybe I'm just a gentleman?"

I rolled my eyes. "Joseph Chase, you are known around here with the ladies for many things, but being just a nice gentleman isn't really in the cards for you—reputation and all."

"Reputation?" he argued. "Can't a guy just simply be a regular old eager beaver?"

"I'm not saying I don't appreciate your kindness," I argued, holding back a smile. "It's just that I've heard the other ladies talking, and I know about you, Joey."

"Well, I'll be damned." He chuckled. "I have a reputation with the dames."

"Honestly speaking though," I almost whispered. "Why are you being so good to me?"

Joey's eyes met mine, and before he explained, I already knew. "Gerry asked me to take care of you," he said.

I nodded. I had expected as much. "You don't have to, you know."

"I know."

"I can take care of myself."

Joey laughed. "Oh, you are doing a great job with that one."

I rolled my eyes and shoved his shoulder. "Don't be cruel."

"You're cooking with gas, you know!"

"Zip it, Joey Chase." I pretended to punch him.

His expression became softer. "I miss him too, you know."

"I know."

* * *

A WEEK LATER, as I wrote another letter to my husband, I realized I was running out of things to say. All of my questions and worries had gone unanswered for so long that I was starting to lose hope. It was almost easier to imagine that he was dead and wasn't coming home. That thought alone was enough to send me into hysterics once more. I set my pen down and began to seal another envelope through my tears. I felt as though I might be drowning. I pictured myself out at sea with no life vest to speak of, my head plummeting under the water and bobbing back up, hopeful for a breath. That was how not knowing felt. The anticipation was worse than anything I could dream of.

My thoughts were interrupted as Joey entered the cottage. He hung up his hat, coat, and scarf on the hook and hustled toward the kitchen. "It's bloody cold out there!" he exclaimed.

"I've had the fire going all morning," I noted.

The brick fireplace had grown to be one of my favorite things about my apartment on the first floor. No matter how cold and dreary the world had become, I could count on the heat from the burning logs and comfort in the way the orange flames danced.

"I was thinking about it today, and I decided you need to get yourself a Christmas tree."

"A Christmas tree? Why would I do a thing like that? It's only me living here," I argued.

"The Christmas spirit, Gwen."

"I usually love Christmas…"

"You need Christmas stockings as well," he continued, obviously ignoring me.

"Well, I don't have those."

"Didn't anyone ever teach you to knit?"

"Well, yes," I chuckled.

"Then get cracking, young lady." He laughed. "When Gerry comes home, he's going to need himself a Christmas stocking."

LATER THAT DAY, I took his suggestion and bundled up in my coat, hat, scarf, and boots. It was one of the first times I had left the cottage since Gerry's departure other than to mail my letters or go to the lighthouse. Winter by the sea in Maine was arctic. The wind off the coast was piercing enough to freeze my head to the point of becoming agonizing. But not today. Today, I welcomed the cold wind as it furiously met my face. Feeling pain in my physical body that matched the ache in my soul was somehow refreshing.

There were not too many people out and about, and I was thankful for that. There was something peaceful about walking by Long Sands on my own, allowing positive memories in, like the day Gerry proposed, for starters. I purchased the materials needed to knit my Christmas stockings, along with some milk, bread, and other necessary items I had gone without. I wasn't sure I would be getting a Christmas tree anytime soon, but knitting Christmas stockings was one place I could start.

NOW- CASSIDY

CHAPTER EIGHTEEN

I have only been home from my trip into Boston for an hour, and Sean and I are already elbow deep in Grandpa's mystery trunk. He is reading letter after letter aloud, and I am digging through old photographs. Sean is still filthy from rummaging around in the attic, and the U-Haul, parked on the side of the road, remains packed full of boxes.

I get up and grab Sean's beer, sit down beside him, and hand it to him, sipping mine quickly. He hasn't taken his eyes off the letters since he started reading them. I have to hand it to my grandmother. She must have really loved Grandpa. I'm not sure I would have the patience and the discipline to email or even text someone every day, let alone put something in the mail daily.

"Here," I say. "Drink this and take a break."

"Your grandmother married my grandfather," Sean says under his breath.

"Yeah, I guess she did." I laugh again, wide-eyed at the thought of Grandma Gwen locking lips with Grandpa Gerry.

"You look just like her," he says, not removing his eyes

from the photograph. "I guess this explains why Grandpa had a thing for you," he jokes.

"He didn't have a thing for me." I pretend to kick him with my bare foot. "But yes, it explains a lot." I think back to that afternoon in the cottage when Grandpa spilled his coffee and reacted so strongly. "He did call me Dolly," I remember. "But I had never heard Grandma called Dolly before."

"Why do you think he called her that?"

I rub my tired eyes. "I have no idea. I guess there is a lot I don't know about Grandma," I respond with a yawn.

This has been the longest day ever. Retrieving my things from the city was really unpleasant. Emma literally acted as my attorney or my bodyguard. I couldn't tell which. We loaded box after box into the U-Haul this morning, all the while listening to Colton go on about what a horrible person I am while watching us carry things into the truck and not lifting a finger. He was too busy going on and on about timing, his reputation, how seeing me was a waste of his time. I thought Emma might punch him square in the face when I loaded the last box into the truck and he turned to me, looking defeated and humiliated.

"My mother was right about you," he said in a disturbing monotone voice usually saved for serial killers on crime TV. "She said you were crazy. And you know what? She was right."

I had cringed and waited a beat before responding. Of course, he was talking about the condition of my brain following my accident, something the two of us had rarely discussed. I realized then that he was hurting and grasping at ways to hurt me. I decided to take the high road instead of opening my palm and slapping his face like I wanted to.

"I love you, Colton," I had said, looking him straight in the eyes. "I never meant for any of this to happen." With that, I returned his ring to the palm of his hand, closed his fist, and kissed his knuckles.

As if reading my mind or noticing my trance, Sean apologizes for being so obsessed with his new findings and not asking how it went today.

"It's over," I sing. I hold up my naked, diamondless fingers and clap as if congratulating myself.

"Come here." Sean puts his beer to the side and pulls me onto the couch with him. I straddle his torso and wrap my arms around his shoulders, burying my face in his neck, and decide that it's my favorite place to be.

"Are you okay?" he asks. His breath is warm against my ear.

"I will be," I respond with a kiss on his cheek. "It wasn't meant to be."

"Well, this guy here is pretty happy it wasn't."

His comment makes me smile, and for a moment, I do feel a little better. "I'm just glad it's over," I say.

"How was it? Seeing him?"

"Oh, he was a total jerk," I admit.

"How so?" His eyes portray concern, but his frown screams "I'll kick his ass."

"It's fine," I lie.

"What did he say?"

I press my forehead against his and inhale deeply. "He called me crazy."

"Crazy? Why would he..." His voice fades as he meets my stare. I pick up his hand and trace the outline of my scar with his pointer finger.

"I'll kill him," he snaps.

I shake my head and hug him again. "No, don't kill him. He's just hurting."

"Well, he's about to be hurting more."

I laugh. "Okay, tough guy, that's enough."

"Seriously, Cassidy." He takes my face in his hands, and I have nowhere to look but into his dark eyes. "You are not crazy. You are an incredible woman."

"Thank you," I whisper. My lips meet his for a quick kiss, and then we share another embrace. "I do want to keep reading these letters though."

"Why is that?" he asks.

"We need to make sure we aren't related." I laugh.

His lips curl up in a smile, and he playfully chucks a throw pillow at my face. "Not cool." He laughs. "Not cool."

* * *

WE DECIDE to leave the U-Haul packed until tomorrow so that we can continue reading Grandma's letters to Grandpa. I find myself feeling very emotional as I listen to my grandmother write about love and loss. It shakes me to my core to think about how she must have felt, not knowing if Gerry was dead or alive. I remember how hard it was to lose my mother, father, and grandmother at the same time, but at least I wasn't left without answers. And why wasn't he writing back?

I consult Google about the process of mail during World War II and learn that at the start of the war, the mail was slow. Some soldiers received it, and some didn't. That could make sense, couldn't it?

She was utterly transparent in each and every letter, and I envy the way she was able to be so open about her feelings. She really did love him very much, which blows my mind, because as her granddaughter, I never even knew this relationship existed. It didn't surprise me that Grandma had such a big secret. She was often full of surprises.

There is also not much mention of Grandma Gwendoline having any friends at all in the letters. I feel sorry for her that she didn't have a girlfriend to share her time with. I think about Emma and appreciate her immensely. I never would have made it through today without her. Grandma didn't write about any friends at all, actually. She just rambled about memories she and Grandpa had shared. She wrote about their engagement, and I laugh out loud, picturing my grandmother standing in the middle of Long Sands with a man in front of her on one knee and then the two of them rolling in the tide, fully dressed. Of course my grandmother got engaged in the ocean. I wouldn't have expected anything less from her.

WINTER OF 1943- GWENDOLINE

CHAPTER NINETEEN

*O*ur Christmas stockings were hung over the fireplace. They weren't perfect, but they were ours: a red one for me and a green one for Gerry. Joey kept his word and cut me down the perfect little Christmas tree. What it lacked in decoration it made up for in spirit and a lot of silver tinsel.

Christmas had come and gone, and we were well into January. I didn't want to take down my stockings and my tree. It made me happy to have holiday spirit in my apartment. As I finished up another letter to my husband, I cried my usual tears. This time in my letter, I told him the story of the day he proposed to me. I wrote of my wishes that he stay well and healthy. If there was any way he could send word of his well-being, it would make me the happiest girl alive.

Newspapers and the radio became my lifelines. I searched through photographs and articles, hoping for some sign that Gerry was okay. I listened to broadcasts about Navy ships and battles and bombings and cringed each time there was mention of casualties. I could sense that this was the case with Joey as well. I had asked him to pick up sardines and saltine crackers, as I couldn't listen to the radio without them.

"What are you knitting now?" Joey asked. He sat by the fire, sipping his tea.

"Not sure yet. Just knitting."

"I had fun last night."

I looked up from my project and nodded.

Last night, Joey had taken me into town to the piano bar overlooking Short Sands. He convinced me that getting out of the house would be healthy for me. I was pretty sure he and my mother were in cahoots in persuading me to get decked out for a night on the town. I agreed and made it clear to Joey that it really was good for my soul. After a couple of after-dinner drinks, I'd felt the best I had felt in months. We had talked and laughed together. When I'd had too much to drink, we went dancing and put on quite the show with our jitterbug routine. And after a couple more drinks, I reminded him over and over again that I was a married woman. He had laughed and told me that he would pay Gerry back in beer when he came home.

The next morning, however, I felt nothing but guilt and shame. *Really, Gwendoline? Going out with another man and getting drunk while your husband fights in a war? Really?*

I dropped one of my knitting needles and bumped my head on the coffee table as I reached for it. "Ouch," I mumbled.

"Are you okay?" Joey asked.

"Yes. I just bumped my head."

"Let me see."

"I'm fine."

He ignored this and scooted over to me on the couch. "If you could just let me look at it…"

"I said I'm fine!" I swatted his hand away from my face in

annoyance. I wasn't sure who was more surprised, Joey or me. What was coming over me?

Joey jumped back with his palms in front of him.

"I'm sorry," I sobbed.

"Don't be sorry, Gwen."

I hated that I liked when he called me Gwen. I hated even more how much I was starting to care for him. He scooted over next to me again and hugged me. It wasn't our first embrace.

"I'm sorry," I said again. I wiped my eyes with my favorite blue handkerchief.

"No," he said firmly, taking my chin in his hand. "Don't be sorry. You have nothing to be sorry for."

"I'm a terrible person. You have been nothing but good to me...and Gerry..."

"Gwendoline." He stopped and bit his lower lip then ran his fingers through the back of his hair in frustration. "You are not a horrible person. You are an incredible woman."

I shook my head, and he argued once more. This time, I allowed my needles and yarn to fall on the floor, and my empty hands held his face. He did the same, holding mine in his hands. We sat there on the couch, facing each other, holding on for what felt like dear life. It felt like hours passed, and I gave up, succumbing to the uninvited tears.

I wasn't wise beyond my years, but I knew enough to understand that there were moments in our lives that defined us, split-second decisions that could characterize who we were. For Joey Chase and me, that was that moment. After spending a few more breaths staring into his eyes and realizing how empty they looked and realizing for the first time just how blue they were, how much I liked the way he looked at me, how good it felt to be touched, well, I lost track of who I was and what was right. I pulled Joey Chase's face toward mine in one of the longest, most passionate kisses of my life, and he didn't pull away.

Something about kissing Joey felt so familiar and so right that I was immediately taken by surprise and flooded with feelings of guilt and dishonor but at the same time charged with an energy I couldn't explain.

"I'm sorry," I whispered, pulling back and panicking.

"No," Joey said. "Gwen…" His words were lost, but I didn't need them. His eyes spoke for us both. The intensity in his embrace as he pulled me close again was enough.

I gave up. I couldn't hold on anymore. I needed to feel something…anything…anything at all. He kissed me again, and this time, my body came alive. My fingers ran through his hair, and my lips danced with his, connecting like we had always done in the past while goofing off with our dancing. But this was different. We were in my bedroom before I could comprehend what was happening.

I couldn't remember every detail of that night, but I did remember my fingers in his hair and his body on top of mine. Everything about him felt safe and right. I felt protected, immune to the pain of the outside world, as if nothing could hurt me if I stayed right there in that moment with him. In his arms, with his body inside mine, I was free from the prison I had created for myself. I was alive.

When it was over, I waited for the shame and the regret and the devastation that should have immediately followed such an unforgivable act. But they didn't come. Instead, I welcomed the idea of possibility, the idea that it might be okay to move on. I hoped that maybe my life wasn't actually over after all. I told myself that this was what Gerry would want for me. Or at least that lie could help me get through life without him one day at a time.

* * *

THE NEXT MORNING, I awoke like I usually did, hoping this season was simply a nightmare. Only this day was different. On this particular morning, I was not alone. I propped myself up on my elbows and watched Joey sleep for about ten minutes, admiring his features as if I had never gotten to see them before. I secretly hoped that I might get to see more of him in this way. His strong eyes were soft while he slept. His cheekbones were more defined than I'd ever paid attention to. I lay back down and curled up next to him, inhaling deeply, appreciating the warmth of his body, and falling back to sleep once more.

I awoke sometime later to a knock at the door.

"Gwendoline, dear, are you there? It's Mrs. Anderson."

Holy hell! Mrs. Anderson!

"Joey!" I whispered.

"Good morning, beautiful," he said.

"Joey, it's Mrs. Anderson."

"Gerry's mother?" He jumped up in alarm and began scurrying around for his clothes.

"Gwendoline, honey, I have news! You have a letter!"

I had a letter? A letter from Gerry? I had dreamed of this moment over and over in my mind, and not once did I picture it happening with a naked Joey Chase scurrying around my bedroom. Joey, naked, in my room. What had I done? All of the feelings surrounded me at once. Nausea swept over my own naked body. I grabbed my robe and pulled it on. I'd slept with Joey Chase last night, and now there was a letter from Gerry? Gerry wasn't dead.

"I'll be right there!" I shouted. I put my finger over my mouth to say "Quiet" and closed my bedroom door behind me. I hurried over to the front door and opened it quickly for Mrs. Anderson.

"Seriously, Gwendoline, I was freezing out here."

"Sorry," I said. "I was asleep."

"It's okay! You got a letter from Gerry! We got one too! He's okay! He's in France, and he is healthy and doing well."

She hugged me tightly, and my knees trembled. Could she smell Joey on me? Humiliation and worry taunted me from my toes to the deepest part of my soul.

"Here," she said, tucking the letter into the pocket of my robe. "Make yourself some tea and read this. You are going to feel so much better after you do."

DECEMBER 10, 1942

My Dearest Dolly,

Today was the first day we got our mail. Some of the guys received a letter or two or even a package. But it confirmed what I already knew: that I have the best wife in the world. Holy mackerel, Dolly, you have been writing to me every day! The guys are so jealous, especially a friend of mine who didn't get any letters. Another guy, Lawrence, I've gotten to know just found out that his dame is sleeping with his brother. Can you believe it? The scandal! I haven't even counted all of your letters, let alone read them, but I want you to know that I am okay. It hasn't been easy, but I'm getting it done, and I will be home to you before you know it. Merry Christmas, my Gwendoline.

Love, Gerry

* * *

I SPENT the next couple of weeks avoiding Joey Chase. I told myself that nothing had happened between us. I blamed everything that happened on a moment of weakness.

The mail kept coming, bringing letter after letter from Gerry. The mailman said that it could take up to four weeks for me to get a letter from France. There were stories of being out at sea, some exciting and some devastating.

Knowing he was alive was an answer to my prayers, but I couldn't shake the feelings I was experiencing. I was disgusted with my behavior, but at the same time, I couldn't avoid falling back into daydreams about Joey. Some were daydreams and some were nightmares. It had been one thing when there was a possibility that my husband was dead. But now?

Avoiding Joey was problematic, as he lived on the third floor and I on the first. There were awkward moments, like when we ran into each other while getting the mail. Other times, I sat on the balcony of the first floor, and I could hear him talking with Mr. Anderson over cigars and could smell the smoke as if they were inches from me.

He was also playing music on his record player now more than ever. His Glenn Miller records played over and over again. In some ways, I hoped he was thinking of me, but in other ways, I prayed he would move on. I closed my eyes and sang along to his music, picturing us together on the dance floor, and hated myself for it.

But I couldn't see him. I started missing our friendship almost as much as I missed my husband. I detested eating breakfast by myself. I didn't like making my own tea. I was furious with myself for allowing things to get out of hand with my friend. Gerry had trusted me, and he had even asked Joey to take care of me, but I was pretty sure that this was not what he'd meant.

I loved my husband. I needed him to come home more than anything. The shame and the fear of what I had done with Joey slowly ate away at me, and I started hating the woman I had become. Would I ever be able to look Gerry in the eyes again? Looking at myself in the mirror was becoming impossible not only because the eyes that stared back at me were angry and accusatory but because the secret I was carrying couldn't stay a secret for much longer.

* * *

IT WASN'T until the nausea set in and I was convincingly late that I allowed myself to believe that I was pregnant. It wasn't until I started to show that I went to see my mother. She was the only one I could confide in, the only one that I would tell. Nobody else could know my secret.

"Momma!" I had bolted into her arms like a frightened child the second she opened the door on that cool spring morning. My plan had been to enter our little cottage quickly, afraid to be spotted in my condition.

"I'm pregnant, Momma," I cried, not even making it completely inside.

"Gwendoline, dear," she gasped. She placed one of her hands on my abdomen and the other behind my head as I cried.

"What am I going to do?" I wailed over and over again.

My mother pulled me close to her and squeezed me tight. "Shhh, darling. Calm down. It's okay."

"No it isn't!" I cried.

"It's all going to be all right," she said as she stroked my hair and rubbed my back. "We will figure it out."

"How?"

"These kinds of things happen all the time, Gwendoline," she said. "We will get through it."

I sat down on her sofa, and she put some water on for tea. "First things first," she instructed. "We need to get you to a doctor. I need to make sure everything is good with my baby and her baby."

"Oh, Momma." My voice caught in my throat. Why was she being so good to me? Could she believe the baby was Gerry's? Clearly she understood that the timing of this was off, right? "Momma, the baby..."

"Now, now, dear, there is no use in going down that

rabbit hole right now. You need to stay calm," she said. "Here, drink your tea."

I took this little attempt at avoidance as an understanding that she knew what was going on. She was making this too easy for me. I wanted to be reprimanded, scolded, shamed. Wasn't that what I deserved?

"People are going to talk," I whispered. "Gerry has been gone since September. Here it is almost March!"

My mother put her hand on my knee, and her eyes met mine with a serious spark of hope. "You leave all of that to me," she said. "Now, what you should be scared of more than anything is what your daddy is going to do to that Joey Chase with his shotgun."

May 21, 1943

Dear Gerry,

I have news! You are going to be a father! Can you believe it? My mother brought me to see the doctor, and he confirmed it. I'm very far along and wanted to tell you for some time now, but I didn't want to get your hopes up until I knew the baby is healthy. I hope this news finds you safe. Come back to us soon!

Dolly

* * *

As the months passed and the chill left the air, my spirits grew happier and my belly grew larger. My heart broke when my fingers grew swollen and I needed to remove my wedding ring. Mrs. Anderson and my mother were busy knitting and shopping, cooking for me and clucking over me like mother hens do to their chicks. Only my mother knew my secret. If Mrs. Anderson figured it out, she didn't let on. In just a few short weeks, I would leave York Beach and go upstate to visit my mother's sister and her family. I was already showing, and although my gowns were loose enough to hide most of me, it wouldn't be long until others started noticing and talking and whispering about the timing, already hungry for a scandalous distraction.

Those few weeks felt shorter than I anticipated, and as my departure grew near, I started to become sorrowful. Aunt Shirley didn't live near the ocean, and I wondered how I would actually be able to breathe air that lacked salt. My swollen, pregnant ankles felt great relief from the coolness of the water. I had been spending my time at the beach again and finding some comfort in what my mother had said, that maybe things might just be okay.

I stared out at the sea and wondered if I would ever look at it in the same way. I used to be able to look out to the ocean and dream. Now all I saw was Gerry, out there some-where, heartbroken over a choice I made—that I needed to make, really. I tried and tried to justify my choice, but in the end, it was the path I had taken, and I would need to live with it. I thought of Robert Frost, Gerry's favorite poet, and his poem about a road diverging into two. Robert Frost claimed to have taken the correct path, or at least the one less traveled. Where did my choice leave me? Leave us?

"I figured I might find you here."

Startled, I turned around, not sure who to expect. "Joseph," I said with a nod.

"Gwen."

"It's Gwendoline," I corrected.

"Fine, Gwendoline," he affirmed, walking up behind me and stepping over the large rocks that surrounded the light-house. "Are you ever going to talk to me again?"

My gaze didn't leave the horizon. "I'm a married woman."

"You are a married woman carrying my child," he said.

I pulled him away from the crowds and waited until we were alone before drawing back my hand and, with full force, smacking him straight in the face.

He stood there, stunned, shaken to the core. "What was that?"

The blood rose to my cheeks, and I could feel my face turning as red as my hair. I pointed my finger at him, and my words came out in piercing, threatening sobs. "You listen to me, Joseph Chase. This is Gerry's baby. This is not your baby," I spat. "How dare you even think to mention otherwise."

He put his hands in his pockets and stared down at the ground. My tears blurred my vision, and I was thankful I couldn't clearly see his eyes.

"Gwen...Gwendoline...I..." He leaned in closer, his face inches from my ear.

"Gerry is my husband," I whispered.

"I truly care for you."

I nodded in agreement. "I'm thankful for you, Joey, I am." The tears fell freely now. "But there is no other way. This is how it needs to be." I stepped back, being sure to keep my distance as people walked by us and tourists ran about.

"That night with you, Gwen." He stepped closer. "I will never forget that."

I looked away and had nothing left to say. He kissed my forehead and placed a hand on my swollen belly. My knees were weak, and my aching heart was too much to handle.

"Please don't," I begged. My heart broke as I saw him crumble. "People are watching us."

"I will always love this child, even if it won't be mine. I will always love you." His voice broke between words. "If this is what you want, I will do it. But I will always love you."

"I'm leaving," I snapped. "I'm going away for a while.

Leave us alone." I pushed his hand off my stomach and marched away, hoping at that moment that my night with Joey had, in fact, been the biggest mistake of my entire life and that walking away from him in this moment was not.

I took the road less traveled by
And that is what made the difference

* * *

JUNE 18, 1943

MY DEAREST GWENDOLINE, you have made me the happiest man alive. I didn't think it was possible for you to make me any happier than you already have. Hot dog! A baby! I think we will have a boy. What do you think? What are we going to name him (or her)? I can't wait until I can come home and be with you. Make sure you get rest, and have Momma cook you up some extra soup to keep you both growing strong. I'm sure you look beautiful. Maybe you could take a photograph so I can see what you look like.

I LOVE YOU, my Dolly, forever and always.
　　Gerry

NOW- JOEY CHASE

CHAPTER TWENTY

$\mathcal{I}$ spend my time at the piano bar often. It's not because I love the atmosphere; college kids and tourists today aren't necessarily my cup of tea. But every so often, the right song comes on and the right intoxicated wise guy gets up to sing, and I am taken back in time, like I'm sucked up into some kind of time machine and transported back to that first night I spent out on the town with Gwendoline. I can see the polka dots on her dress and the shiny pearl earrings and red lipstick. I remember the way her eyes locked with mine when we danced. Her smile was as soft as a gentle sea breeze. And just as quickly as I am there, I am gone, probably because I am old and tired, and a man approaching one hundred years old really has no business being out at a piano bar in the middle of the night alone.

I take the final sip of my drink and pay the tab. I haven't done much drinking lately, as the doctor told me a man my age should be thankful he still has a liver. But it has sure been a confusing summer, to say the least. I had to handle the Cassidy situation carefully. When she showed up again, I wasn't sure what to do. I played it nice and cool with Sean, but the situation itself is just impossible. That was when I started coming here again. That was when I started needing to remember how things used to be, and it hurts a great deal.

My cell phone is buzzing next to me, and I strain my eyes to read the texts I have managed to miss. As much as I love modern technology, sometimes I miss just being able to sit and eat my dinner without people having access to me twenty-four, seven. It's Sean Anderson. I haven't heard much from him since Cassidy's return to the cottage in an effort to keep my distance.

Sean: You around?
Joey: I'm down at the bar. Everything ok?
Sean: Could you stop by at some point?
Joey: Tonight?
Sean: If you can.
Joey: Sure Sean, I'll be over soon.

* * *

WHEN I GET to the cottage, I am surprised to see the U-Haul parked in front. I look up to the third floor of the house and marvel at the fact that not much has changed. I am glad to be able to keep the cottage going for Gerry. What I'm not happy about is the mess that we have found ourselves in, and I have a feeling that shit is going to hit the fan, so to speak, sooner than later.

Cassidy and Sean sit curled up on the sofa with papers spread out on the floor and a large green trunk open on the coffee table. Empty beer bottles line the counters.

"Are you moving in for good?" I joke.

Neither of them laugh. They look tired—exhausted, really. Cassidy twirls the red strands in her ponytail around her finger. The expression on her face tells me she means business. She looks just like her grandmother, and the resemblance is eerie.

"What's all this?" I ask, realizing that they don't need me to fix a pipe or a leak in the ceiling and realizing instead that they have found Gerry's trunk. This worries me for Cassidy. It might be too much too soon. Nothing in those letters will have anything to do with me at least. I know because I have read them all over and over again.

"I found this in the attic," Sean explains.

"Gerry's things," I affirm. How could I be so careless?

"Yes," Cassidy agrees. "Grandpa's things. But the thing is...these letters...they are from..."

"Your grandmother," I interrupt. "The letters are from your grandmother, Gwendoline."

She jumps to her feet. "You knew her?"

I nod. "Yes, I knew your grandmother well." *Really well*, I think.

"Have you known about this the whole time?"

I nod. "I didn't think it was my place to tell."

"What the hell, man?"

"I'm...I'm sorry, Sean," I say as I sit in Gerry's chair, wishing I could light up a cigar with him like the old days. "Take it easy on the old man. I'm practically a hundred years old. And also, I miss your grandfather every day."

Cassidy and Sean stare at me with awkward expressions. They look to each other and then to me as if they aren't sure who should speak first.

"Yes, Gerry and your grandmother, Gwendoline, were married," I affirm.

"And they had a baby," Cassidy interrupts. "Was the baby my mother? I never knew my grandfather, so it would make sense."

I stare up at the ceiling, unsure what to say.

"Joey?" Sean asks.

"I don't think this is my place," I explain as honestly as I can, choosing my words carefully.

Cassidy jumps to her feet. "Not your place? Then whose place is it? They are dead!" she cries. "Sean's grandpa and my grandma, my mom and dad." A slight sob escapes from within her, and I feel terrible. I am at a loss for words, and the situation is lose-lose.

"I'm sorry," I whisper. "I wouldn't even know where to begin."

"But I—"

I hold up my hand to cut her off. "But I can try."

CHAPTER TWENTY-ONE

*I*t had been weeks since we were notified of Gerry's injuries. His mother phoned me as soon as she found out. I packed up my things immediately from Aunt Shirley's, where Elizabeth and I had been staying. I gathered our necessary items and got us settled back at the cottage on the first floor. Gerry would be coming home soon. It was too early to tell just how bad his injuries were, but the United States Navy had already awarded him a Purple Heart for his fortitude.

My heart raced with anticipation. Mr. and Mrs. Anderson suspected that he would be dropped off at the cottage, possibly with little to no warning. For this reason, every day, I woke up and put on one of my best dresses, kept my hair pinned back perfectly, and applied lipstick multiple times a day. Elizabeth was also dressed in her best clothes just in case this was the day Daddy came home. She looked splendid in anything she wore, really. My favorite was a little green silk ruffled dress that made her tiny red pigtails seem even brighter, if that was at all possible.

A knock at the door startled me, and I looked up, hopeful

that it could be Gerry. But it wasn't. I stood up instantly, shocked to see Joey Chase at the door.

"May I come in?" he asked.

"Joseph Chase, what in the name..." I pulled Elizabeth up onto my hip and backed away from the door.

"Calm down now, Gwen," he whispered.

"Calm down? My husband could be here any minute," I said. "Don't tell me to calm down."

"I'm sorry," he replied. "I know that Gerry is coming home soon. That is exactly why I'm here."

I stared at him suspiciously. "You aren't here to see Gerry," I accused.

His eyes met mine. Big. Blue. Elizabeth's eyes. I looked away.

"Please go."

Joey ignored my request and closed the door behind him. "I just came to give my best wishes to your family, I promise."

Of course he wanted to see his friend. Had I become so selfish and obsessed with the anticipation of being reunited with my husband that I had forgotten about Joey's relationship with Gerry? It appeared to be the case. I nodded, fighting the urge to hand him our daughter, but instead, I squeezed her tighter to my hip.

"Well, if you really are here for Gerry, you may as well make yourself comfortable. Can I make you some tea?"

* * *

AN HOUR LATER, Joey sat on the sofa, bouncing Elizabeth on his knee, the joy on his face bittersweet. I sipped my tea and begged myself to be strong. What we were doing was best for everyone. I loved my husband, but watching Joey with my baby didn't just warm my heart, it ignited it. This was the way it needed to be. I tried hard to ignore how handsome this man was, but it wasn't easily done. His hands looked strong around the tiny ruffles of the baby's green dress. One small black-and-white saddle shoe had fallen off, but neither of them seemed to care. She laughed and smiled at Joey as he bounced her again, singing "Pony Boy," a song that I remembered my own father singing to me. Her smile was one of joy, and his was simply awestruck.

" Gwen...she is just..."

"Thank you," I replied, not allowing him to finish his sentence.

"She must be what, about eighteen months?"

I looked at him sternly. "Yes. Between you and me, she was born October 15. But the rest of the world will believe her birthday to be August 25."

I studied his eyes for any judgment but found little evidence of any. My mother's plan hadn't been perfect by any means, but it got the job done. Being away at Aunt Shirley's for the duration of my pregnancy and for the first year or so of Elizabeth's life had been a struggle to say the least. However, it was the only way to ensure that nobody would figure out that Gerry was not Elizabeth's father.

"Can I come back again? And see her?" he asked.

"I…"

We were interrupted by the sound of cars honking and voices cheering outside the cottage windows.

"It's him, Gwendoline!" Mrs. Anderson shouted from the upstairs porch. "It's Gerry! He's home!"

"Gerry." My voice caught in my throat.

I looked from Elizabeth to Joey and back and then stood up like a madwoman, pacing in circles in front of them. I should have been happy. Of course I was happy. I stopped in my tracks and stared at Joey like a drowning person waiting to be rescued. *Tell me what to do*, I thought.

As if reading my mind, he stood from the sofa with the

baby, his face inches from me. The ache in my heart took my breath away.

"Here," Joey whispered. "Let her meet her father."

My words were lost as Elizabeth wrapped one of her little arms around my neck, and her tiny fingers grabbed at my face. One hand landed on my face and the other on Joey's.

"Pony Boy!" Elizabeth sang.

"That's right! Pony Boy!" he repeated.

Our eyes locked again, and his were a window into the sadness of his soul.

"Go!" he says, turning away from both of us, rubbing his hands through his hair.

I nodded and hurried outside, leaving Joey Chase standing in my kitchen with his hands in his pockets, holding back his tears.

Outside in the streets, people cheered, whistled, and hollered. I looked around but was overwhelmed with the scene. My heart raced, and I panicked as people turned to blurry figures in my mind. My thoughts spun around as if I were on a carousel at the fair.

And then I heard him.

"Dolly!"

I turned around quickly, spotting him on the other side of the road. "Gerry!" "Gerry!"

I ran as fast as my legs would carry me. Gerry, in uniform, leaned on a pair of wooden crutches in front of his bus, surrounded by neighbors, friends, and family.

I tried calling out again, but my voice caught somewhere between my throat and my lips.

Mrs. Anderson grabbed my hand, pulling us over to him. My lips found his in a kiss before my words could find meaning. Then my free hand found his face. The weight of the world melted off my shoulders, and I wanted to stay in that moment forever.

"Are you okay?" I asked in between kisses.

"I am now, Dolly."

"Don't ever leave me again."

He laughed and kissed me again, pulling back only to admire Elizabeth. "She's beautiful!"

"Elizabeth," I said between sobs. "Elizabeth, meet your daddy."

* * *

AT FIRST, our reunion was everything I could have imagined. Mrs. Anderson and I cooked a feast on the second floor—a roast with potatoes and carrots, Gerry's favorite. Joey Chase, Gerry, and Mr. Anderson sat in their recliners with their cigars, Gerry's leg propped on a stool. Although the awkwardness with Joey was overwhelming, I decided I might as well get used to it. Besides, seeing the three men together again made my heart happy.

I was sure that once I got Elizabeth to bed, he would already be sleeping, but he wasn't. He sat up in our bed with his crutches leaned against the wall next to him, his shirt off already and cozy under our covers. I climbed into bed next to him, wearing my favorite nightgown, which I'd saved for weeks upon notice of his return, not able to believe that he was really here.

"What are you thinking about, Dolly?" he whispered.

"You."

"Little old me?" he joked.

"I just can't believe you are really here."

"Well, I am," he whispered as his finger traced my mouth.

"I prayed for this moment." I leaned forward and kissed him again, unable to think about anything other than my perfect husband being home and in my bed.

He tried to sit up and roll onto his side, but he winced in

pain. I held up my hand and told him to stay still. He didn't need to tear his stitches open and be shipped back to the hospital. He complied and relaxed as I traced his neck and chest with my lips. I pulled my nightgown over my head, tossed it to the side, and carefully slid my body on top of his just the way I remembered he liked it. We kissed and made love all night, stopping only for the moments in which my joy mixed with sadness and the tears on my pillow reminded me of the shame I was hiding and how much I hated myself for it.

* * *

I WASN'T the only one battling demons. Night after night, Gerry awoke from nightmares and sweats that soaked the entire bed. He was home for months before the drinking started, but once it started, it didn't stop. He had always enjoyed a Scotch with his cigar or a beer when we went dancing, but this was different. He was using the drink to take away his physical pain and probably emotional terrors as well. Deep inside, I knew there was much more to it. When he woke during the night, screaming about what he had witnessed overseas, I realized that he was using his drinking to actually try and erase his memory. I had tried talking to him about it, but as time went on, he became angry and distant to me and even to Elizabeth.

I had arranged a meeting with Joey at the lighthouse to see if he would spend some time with Gerry and try to help him through this. The two of us had sat on a bench over-looking the waves as they crashed on the mountains of rocks surrounding the Nubble. He held Elizabeth on his lap and kissed the top of her little red head as she slept.

"I just don't know how to help anymore," I confessed. "It's like he is an entirely different person now."

"Maybe try and give it time," Joey suggested.

"It's just that…" I couldn't tell anyone just how bad it had gotten with Gerry. I knew he was struggling with his memories from the war. But did that make it right to mistreat his wife and daughter?

"Sometimes men come home different than they were when they left, Gwen. It's just the way it is. He'll come around."

I found comfort in resting my head on his shoulder while he continued holding Elizabeth in his arms, appreciating the quiet and stillness of the night.

THAT NIGHT, Joey tried talking with Gerry, but it was no use. By the time we started dinner, he was already down a bottle of gin and couldn't even form his words correctly. Joey tried making light of the situation by bouncing Elizabeth on his knee and singing "Pony Boy." She clapped and sang along happily.

"Well, ain't that precious," Gerry had slurred from the kitchen table, where his head was barely up off the surface.

"Uncle Joey is pretty stellar," he had responded.

Gerry laughed a wicked laugh that I couldn't recognize and would have liked to forget. "*Uncle Joey?*" He laughed again.

"What's so funny?" I asked. "You and Joey are good friends and all. He can't be her uncle?"

"That's cute, Dolly."

"What's cute?"

He picked his head up off the table and covered his face with his hands. "Uncle Joey. We all know he isn't the baby's uncle. Elizabeth, baby, just call him Daddy."

NOW- CASSIDY

CHAPTER TWENTY-TWO

"Joey," I start, but then I stop. Then I start again. "Joey, are you telling us that you and my grandmother had a child together?"

"Yes." He nods, practically chewing off his bottom lip in an effort to choose the right words.

"My mother?"

"Well, if your mother was Elizabeth Ellis, then yes."

I study him carefully for a beat, realizing that this means Joey is my grandfather.

"What happened after my grandfather found out?" Sean asks. His expression is darker than usual. Of course he would be feeling defensive for Grandpa. I don't blame him for this at all.

"Well," Joey begins, "Gerry's drinking got much worse before it got better. Gwen and the baby moved back up north with her Aunt Shirley, and shortly after that, they moved to the city."

"Boston," I affirm. "My mother was raised in Boston."

"That's correct," Joey agrees.

I think about this for a moment, and suddenly I am very

159

sad. My grandmother ended up alone? And that's why I never met my grandfather? I wipe a tear away from my eye and study Joey.

"So my grandmother ended up alone? It's just so awful."

"Those times were hard times," he confirms. "But she didn't end up alone. I can promise you that."

"What do you mean?" I can't think of anyone my grandmother ever talked about. I always knew she loved my grandfather, but she never talked about him. Why can't I remember anything about my grandfather?

"She didn't end up alone," he repeats.

I look at him in confusion. "But you said..."

"Listen, kids, this old man has had enough for tonight," he says. "Unless you plan on carrying me all the way home to Wells, I should get going."

* * *

It is approaching two in the morning, and Sean and I both lie awake, restless. Joey promised to come back in the morning with more information. I could tell that we exhausted him with our questions, accusations, and obviously judgmental reactions. It was a lot to take in. Of course, I didn't know who my grandfather was, but I never in a million years would have suspected it was Joey Chase, the man taking care of the cottage.

And if I feel this way, then how is Sean feeling? He had explained to me, as we were getting into bed, that he had known his grandmother well. He had spent lots of time with her right here on this beach at this cottage. She had passed away from an illness after Sean graduated high school, and then shortly after that, Sean's parents had moved out west, leaving him to take care of Grandpa.

I study Sean as he lies next to me, staring up at the ceiling, eyes wide open. As eager and excited as I am to find out more about my grandmother and my mother, I can't ignore the fact that my heart is racing just from lying next to him. The blanket only covers a portion of his naked chest, and one of his arms is behind his head. *Sean Anderson, you are gorgeous*, I think. I lean closer and kiss his cheek, taking in the scent of my shampoo, which he borrowed in the shower.

"What are you thinking about?" I whisper, continuing to kiss his forehead.

Sean shrugs and locks his gaze on the ceiling. "What am I not thinking about?" He laughs and rolls onto his side so we are facing one another. He grabs my hand and kisses it. Then he pulls me closer, reaching around my waist with his arm and squeezing me against him.

"It's a lot to take in," I whisper back in between kisses.

He nods and pulls back from me. "I guess I feel sorry for Grandpa."

"I do too," I agree.

"I guess it's all so crazy that this whole universe existed and we had no idea it happened. That these two people had this whole life together, and then it just ended. It's like they erased it."

I pull him close to me and nuzzle my head into the crook of his neck and sigh. "At least we aren't related," I joke.

He laughs and reaches around my waist, scooping me up on top of him. His hands warm the small of my back.

"I guess what I'm trying to say is that it could have been us."

"What do you mean?"

"I mean, we met here on this same beach. That summer with you, Cassidy, was the best summer of my life."

"And we just...ended it," I say.

"Exactly. It could have been us. Cass, the thought of never seeing you again...how could I have been so careless?"

"But it's not us," I reassure him. "Plus, we were just kids back then."

We kiss, and my hair seems to surround him. It's in his face and over his eyes, but he doesn't brush it away. Our kisses grow more passionate, and I know I should keep my eyes closed, but I need to see him. I need to watch the intensity in his face as he pulls me tighter, his sweatpants pressing hard against my shorts. I watch his lips curve in his crooked smile as he moves his hands under my waistband. He explores further and seems to hit all the right places without any effort at all.

* * *

THE NEXT MORNING, I wake up later than normal and find Sean missing from bed. I roll over and pick up my cell phone to check my texts. Sure enough, there is a message from him.

Sean: Good morning beautiful. Joey texted me and asked me to meet him for breakfast. I hope you don't mind. I'll bring you home a latte?

I swipe out of the text, a little irritated that they are continuing this conversation without me. After all, it does involve my grandmother, and Joey is my grandfather. But if this is how we will get Joey to open up, then this is what we have to do. Besides, it has been a while since I have had a morning to myself.

Cassidy: I never say no to coffee. (heart emoji)

* * *

I SPEND the morning cleaning up the cottage, catching up on dishes and laundry, and showering. I toss on a favorite shirt of mine that Emma once gave me for my birthday. On it is a little gingerbread man with gumdrop eyes and a big smile. The caption reads, "Gingers have more fun." I pair it with my denim cutoffs. I toss my wet hair up into a messy bun on the top of my head and decide to hit the beach for a while.

It's a different feeling now as I stroll through town. I'm picturing Grandma walking the same path, sitting on the same benches, looking for sea glass, getting engaged. This is the same sea that she stood in when Gerry proposed to her and the same shore where she stood, allowing the cold water to catch her tears, later on. It sounds as if she carried the shame of her actions for the rest of her life. There is no doubt in my mind that she loved Sean's grandpa, Gerry. But did she love Joey the same way? Joey, my mother's father, my grandfather. I reach into my purse to grab some Advil as I feel a headache coming on.

WHEN I RETURN to the house, Sean is waiting for me, and to my surprise, Emma's car is parked at the curb behind our still-to-be-unpacked U-Haul.

"Emma?" I call out.

"Cassidy, surprise!"

I'm thankful to see her and find comfort in her smile and laugh. Her black hair is pulled back into two short pigtails, and I am immediately jealous of how put together she can look just by tossing on a pair of leggings, some flip-flops, and an off-the-shoulder T-shirt.

"What are you doing here?" I ask.

"What, I can't stop by to see my best friend?"

"Of course you can! You just don't usually surprise me like this, that's all."

She chuckles for a moment, and I recognize her uncomfortable expression. "Sean…"

"I called her and asked her to come, Cass."

Sean is leaning against the side of the cottage, barefoot and holding my coffee. The way he is looking at me is different, fatigued in a way that I can't explain. A concerned expression clouds his eyes.

"What do you mean, you called her?" I don't try to hide the confusion in my voice. What the hell is going on? What is this about? Why is Sean looking at me that way?

"Here," he says, handing me my coffee and placing his hand on my waist. "Let's go inside. We need to talk."

JOEY CHASE IS SITTING in Grandpa's armchair with his feet up on a hassock. His expression is also one of worry. I wonder if this was the same way he looked at my grandmother when he was so concerned for her. But what do they have to be concerned about now?

Emma takes my hand and leads me to the couch, and I sit between her and Sean.

"Can someone please tell me what is going on here?" I ask. My voice does not sound like my own. "Is this some kind of intervention?" I know I sound sarcastic, but I don't mean to be.

Sean squeezes my shoulder, and Emma turns to me, holding onto both my hands.

"Cassidy," she says. Her tone is even and serious. "Cassidy, we have had this conversation before, but I don't think you were ready to hear it. Julie told us not to push any information on you, that you would have to discover the truth on your own. And it looks like you have, or at least the truth is finding you."

"Julie?" She can't be talking about my therapist.

"Yes, Julie."

"Why were you talking to my therapist?" My mind spirals, my head hurts more, and I grow frustrated. But Emma is right. I don't remember having this conversation, but these feelings are way too familiar.

"You don't remember this, Cassidy, but after your car accident, you were in a coma for months."

What is she talking about? I was never in a coma after the accident. I shake my head. "Months? That can't be true. The accident was in October of senior year. I lived with you and your parents right after the accident."

Emma shakes her head quickly. "That's what you believe to be true, but it's not."

"Emma, what is going on? I lived with you. We went to school together. I went to prom with Kyle. We cheered for football season. We graduated together."

"Yes, you graduated, but that was because you had enough credits to graduate before the accident. You were such an overachiever, Cassidy. You were accepted to college with a full scholarship prior to your accident. You didn't return to high school after it happened." Emma wipes a tear from her eye and holds my hands again.

"This is insane," I argue, releasing her hands.

"Cass, let her explain. It's time you hear this."

"Hear what? That you guys think I'm crazy?" I push Sean's hand off my shoulder and begin to stand. "You knew about this the whole time too?"

"Cassidy, wait," Emma insists. "Just read this."

She hands me a newspaper article, and I unfold it quickly, my hands trembling. I don't remember ever seeing this, but it looks familiar in its own way. The black-and-white photo reveals my father's Honda Accord, wrapped around a large oak tree on Route 1.

. . .

165

OCTOBER 11, 1999

Drunk Driving Accident Leaves Three Dead and Two Injured

Authorities and first responders were called to the scene on Friday at 7:30 p.m. in response to a 911 caller who reported that an SUV swerved into oncoming traffic on Route 1, striking a car and causing it to flip multiple times before landing off the road. The driver, Ronald Quinn (58), and passenger Elizabeth Quinn (56), were reported deceased on the spot. Passenger Cassidy Quinn (17) was airlifted to Boston and is reported to be in ICU in critical condition. Passenger Gwendoline Ellis (74) was treated for minor injuries and released. The driver of the SUV, Kyle Marsh (18), was also reported dead at the scene. Authorities have reported that alcohol was a factor in the accident.

I STARE DOWN at the news article and read it multiple times, hoping that something will start making sense.

"Are you okay?" Sean asks.

I look at him as if he is crazy and roll my eyes. "What the hell is this?"

"It's the news report about what happened the night of your accident," he explains.

I place my face in my hands and wipe away my tears. "It's obviously not real."

"Cassidy...it is real."

"So you're saying that my parents died in the accident but Grandma didn't?"

"Yes," Joey answers. "That is exactly what we are saying."

"And...Kyle Marsh was the drunk driver?" My words catch in my throat, and deep sobs escape from somewhere I don't expect. "How could you guys not tell me?"

Emma wraps me in her arms and pulls me close. "We tried, Cassidy."

"You tried to tell me?"

She nods. "A few times, but it was just too much for you. Your brain couldn't handle the pain. I mean, think about it. Both of your parents died, and it was Kyle's fault. Nobody would be able to deal with that."

"No." I shake my head. "This is ridiculous."

I stand up and walk away from the sofa, but Joey stands up and focuses intensely on my gaze. "Before the accident, Cassidy, you knew me as your grandfather."

"What?"

I'm not processing his words. I feel like I'm in the *Matrix* movie. Everything is happening slowly, and my reality is unfolding around me, melting away forever. What I know to be my truths are the opposite. They are lies. My entire adult-hood has been built on lies.

He chokes up and wipes his tears with his handkerchief. "Cassidy, you used to call me Papa."

Papa. I drop my latte, and the hot, thick liquid splashes on my legs, my toes, and the floor. My head starts to pound, and I need to sit down. I miss the couch and slide to the floor, landing in my coffee mess. It's difficult to hold my head up, so I rest it on my knees, unaware that I am rocking back and forth. I'm crying, or at least I think I am. But even more significant are the memories flooding over me like tidal waves in a storm, knocking me down, allowing me only a second to stand before another crashes. The news of the accident and the deaths of my parents have always been memories, but now, suddenly, it has all come back. And it hurts.

I hear them talking around me, but I can't understand what they are saying. My thoughts take over my body, and I realize now that I am sobbing like a baby, mumbling random things like "Grandma survived the accident" and "Kyle is dead" over and over. Why hadn't I realized Kyle was dead? How could I not know that I missed an entire year of high school? How could these people that call themselves family have lied to me all these years?

Emma convinces me to walk with her to the bathroom and turns on the shower. I slip out of my latte-stained clothes and sit on the shower floor, allowing the hot water to run over my head and wash away my tears. Emma promises me that she will help me clean up my favorite shirt and that it isn't ruined forever. The curtain is closed, but I know she is there. My head pounds harder as the pieces to the puzzle come crashing together from pieces of a mystery into my reality.

My entire high school senior year was a reality that I somehow created in my mind when I was in a coma. I remember waking up in the hospital to my Papa Joey standing over me, crying happy tears that I was finally awake. He was so excited to tell my grandmother. I remember being so happy that she was okay. But when I learned the news of my parents' passing and that it was Kyle Marsh who had driven them off the road and that he died in the process, something stopped working right in my brain. Maybe it was due to the impact of the accident, maybe to the traumatic experience, maybe both. I remember now Julie trying to tell me that my grandmother survived the accident. I told her she was wrong, that Grandma was dead. Papa Joey tried calling me, but I didn't recognize him.

"You tried to tell me a bunch of times," I mumble through the shower curtain.

"Yes, I did." Emma whispered from the other side.

"And Sean?"

"What about him, Cass?"

"Did I already know him too? Before the accident? Or did

we really just meet on the beach that day?" I realize now what a coincidence it really was.

"As far as I know, you met him that day," she affirms.

"If Grandma didn't die in the accident, then when did she die?" I know my brain is messed up, but surely I would remember the death of Grandma.

Emma swings the shower curtain open and stares down at my naked, shaking body. "Cassidy," she says, almost laughing. "Your grandma isn't dead. She is very much alive. How many times do I have to tell you?"

NOW- SEAN

CHAPTER TWENTY-THREE

$\mathcal{I}$ hate seeing her this way—so confused, tired, and fragile. I can't even begin to imagine what she is going through. She looks a little better now that she has had some time to process what is happening. She allowed Emma to help her get dressed and cleaned up. Joey made a pot of tea, and the two of them haven't moved from the couch. His arm is draped around her, and she's snuggled against him as if it's the most natural thing on earth. She remembers him now, Papa. How strange it must be that for years, she didn't remember him. Her brain wouldn't let her remember. Too much pain; it had to shut down. I've heard people say things like "You've worried me to death" or "I'm going to lose my mind," but I never actually saw it happen.

Emma and Joey called it dissociative fugue disorder. It is almost like amnesia, but it is brought on by something so traumatic that the brain actually forgets on purpose anything that reminds the person of that hurt. Apparently, Cassidy was so shaken up about the loss of her parents and boyfriend that her brain created an alternate reality for her. Now that she is remembering everything, she is tired, really tired. And she feels really guilty for not seeing her grandmother all this time. The news that she is still alive was a shock to me as well. Apparently she stayed away because the doctors and therapist said it could be too dangerous to try and force Cass to remember. She needed to remember on her own in order to heal.

"Where is Grandma now, Papa?" Cassidy asks Joey.

"She's in an assisted-living facility in Wells."

"Is she sick?"

"No." He chuckles. "Just old like me."

"Well then, why don't you live with her?"

"It's only ten minutes up the road," he answers. "I visit her every day, you know."

Cassidy wipes her eyes with her tissue. "So much time has gone by...so much wasted time."

"She understood, sweetheart."

"Can we see her?" she asks.

"Yes, but first, you need to call your therapist, Julie. We need to make sure we are taking the right steps here. We don't want to lose you again." He kisses the top of her head.

"I'll get your cell phone," I offer.

Julie confirmed that Cassidy's breakthrough is typical for someone dealing with trauma to this degree, and she needs to rest and will be as good as new in no time. She has been cleared to go visit her grandmother, but Julie made Cassidy promise to take it easy and rest. Julie emphasized the importance of continued counseling and scheduled follow-up visits for when Cassidy is back in the city so they can continue their sessions. Julie expressed once again her condolences for the loss of Cassidy's parents and her boyfriend, Kyle Marsh. (I cringed at the term "boyfriend" but let it go considering the circumstances.)

* * *

THE RIDE from York to Wells is short but seems to take forever. Emma drives her car, and Joey sits in the passenger seat. I sit in the back with Cassidy, holding her hand tighter than ever.

"So you guys brought me to York that first summer, hoping I would remember everything?" she asks.

"It was one reason," Emma agrees.

"But you didn't know about Sean and Grandpa at all?"

"No," Emma confirms.

"Papa?" she asks.

Joey nods. "I knew that you might run into Gerry and Sean. What I didn't expect was how quickly you would hit it off. When Gwendoline got word that you two were mucking it up in the cottage right under Gerry's nose, she laughed so hard that her tea almost came out her nose."

"It's weird to think she was right there the whole time when I thought she was dead."

"You know," Joey explains, trying to break the silence, "you and Sean didn't know each other prior to meeting on the beach that day, but you did play together a few times when you were babies."

"Really?" I ask. "I don't remember that."

"Oh yes," he confirms. "Gwendoline used to take Cassidy and Elizabeth to play on the rocks at the lighthouse, and from time to time, Gerry would be there with you, Sean."

"I remember that," I confess.

Cass looks up at me with wide eyes. "You do?"

"I remember it clear as day," I say. And I do. I remember her red pigtails and her freckles and how much she loved bouncing from rock to rock.

"The day on the beach that first summer?"

"I was coming up behind you to say hi." I laugh. "When

you didn't recognize me, I figured you just didn't remember me, and I let it go."

"I must not really remember then," she says.

"You were like two peas in a pod back then," Joey says.

I squeeze her closer to me. "See?" I whisper. "It was meant to be."

NOW- GWENDOLINE

CHAPTER TWENTY-FOUR

I have no complaints about my small apartment. It's bright and colorful, and when the sun shines through my window and warms my face, I feel alive. When I'm feeling up to it, I can sit up in my bed and watch everyone walk by. I love people watching. I create stories in my mind about the men, women, and children outside my window. Some stroll by holding hands, and I like to believe they are in love. And if they aren't, I wish for them the same that I once wished for myself: that they follow their hearts.

She is coming back to me today—my Cassidy. My beautiful, redheaded, green-eyed granddaughter is coming back to me today. Oh, how sad it has been all these years! Sometimes I recall the days when my heart broke because Gerry left for the Navy, and I think that maybe I was being prepared for some of the heartache that we would later face. Of course, losing Elizabeth and Ronnie was the hardest thing I would ever go through. No mother should ever have to bury her own child. And with Cassidy in a coma during the funeral, everything about it was devastating. I never would have made it through without Joey. What a strong man he has been for me. He is good to me; this I know.

There is a knock on the door, and she enters—alone, just as I requested. She looks at me as if she is seeing a ghost. She is not a ghost to me. I have followed her over the years through photographs. I watched her eat pizza on the beach with Sean. But Cassidy was convinced that I was dead, so to see the expression on her face—oh, her beautiful face!—is not a surprise.

"Grandma," she whispers.

"Come here, darling."

"Okay," she whispers through her tears.

"I've missed you."

"I know. I've missed you too."

She wipes her eyes and climbs into my bed with me. She pulls her knees to her chest and buries her face on my bosom just as she did for all of those years we were together—Elizabeth, Ronnie, Joey, Cassidy, and I. We were a family. We still are in a sense.

"I'm sorry," she whispers.

I pull back and pretend to slap her wrist. "None of that," I demand, and she laughs. "None of that was your fault."

"I know, but all these years…"

I hold her hand in mine and notice she isn't wearing an engagement ring. "I thought you were engaged," I say.

"Grandma! How did you know that?"

"I might be nearly one hundred years old, but I can navigate the Facebook too, you know."

She laughs and hugs me tighter. "You really are the best. I've missed you. I miss Mom and Dad."

"They would be so proud of you."

"I have so many questions for you, Grandma."

"Go easy on me. I'm an old lady."

STACY LEE

"Okay." She laughs. "But why didn't you reach out to me after the accident?"

"The doctors said I needed to let you figure it out on your own. You were convinced that I had died in the accident. People told you that I hadn't, so at one point, I tried to call you, but you thought it was a prank. It was best to let it go."

She nods, allowing the memory of this to wash over her. "I'm so sorry."

"Don't be. It wasn't your fault." I kiss the top of her head and wish I could take her pain away.

"His name was Colton," she explains.

"You left him at the altar."

She giggles. "Yes, I did," she says.

"I was there."

"You were there?" she asks.

"I've always been there, my sweet Cassidy."

She cries into my neck, and I am reminded of how she used to get when she was overtired as a toddler. I would sing to her and rock her until she was fast asleep. The memory warms my heart. "Hashtag runaway bride."

She laughs out loud. "It's funny hearing you talk about hashtags."

"He wasn't the one for you."

"I know."

"Is Sean?"

"I think so, Grandma."

"Does he take care of you?"

"Yes," she responds. "One time, I had the flu, and he stayed with me all night."

"He loves you then."

"I love him," she responds. "I remember seeing pictures of your wedding, Grandma. For years, I completely forgot about Papa. But I remember your wedding by the Nubble Lighthouse now. It was beautiful."

"I love your Papa very much."

"I know you do. Grandma, Sean and I found a box of his grandfather's things. There was so much in there...letters from you while he was in the Navy. You told him he was my mother's father."

I nod in agreement. "Yes, all of that is true. I was married to Gerry Anderson before I was married to your papa. I loved them both, you know."

"I was worried Sean and I were related." She laughs.

"Now that would be something!"

"What happened to Sean's grandpa? After he found out that Joey was my mother's dad?"

I am not prepared for this question. She sure has done her share of research. "I mean it when I say that I loved both of those men, Cassidy. Gerry was my first love. I was barely seventeen years old. That night he proposed to me was truly one of the best nights of my life. But the connection I had with Joey Chase...writers can't write about it, singers can't sing about it. It was so real and so unique that I couldn't deny it. I know in my heart I made the right choice."

"I think you did too. Papa is a great man."

"He is," I agree. "He was willing to step back and let Gerry raise your mother. He wanted to honor my wishes no matter what it would cost him. And that only made me fall more in love with him."

"And Gerry?"

I choose my words carefully. "Gerry actually met someone. He was very happy."

"Sean's grandmother Rosemary?"

"Yes."

"Did you know her?"

"Yes, I did. I would bring your mother to York to visit my mother and father. Then later, I would bring you as well."

"You taught me to look for sea glass."

"Of course I did!"

She laughs. "There is still one thing I don't really understand."

"What's that?"

"Why did Sean's grandpa leave me the cottage for one hundred days? Especially if my mother wasn't his baby?"

I kiss the top of her head. "That, my dear, is a completely different story."

WINTER OF 1945- GWENDOLINE

CHAPTER TWENTY-FIVE

*T*he intensity of his gaze as he stared down at the sand between his bare toes would make a person stop and wonder if he was counting the grains. He wasn't counting anything, actually, other than his uninvited tears. He didn't want to cry in front of me. He didn't cry in front of anybody.

I reached out and grasped his hand. The calluses on his fingertips brushed ever so slightly against mine, so slightly that they almost didn't touch. But I knew they were there. I had memorized almost every detail about him: how he awkwardly brushed one hand through the hair on the back of his head when he was nervous, the steady rhythm of his heartbeat when he held me in his arms, the way he smelled first thing in the morning, the look of melancholy in his eyes when I pleaded that he stay.

Except today. Today, there was no begging. No asking. There was just silence. How could there be words on a day like this? There would be no laughing, no dancing, no dreaming of tomorrow. On a day like today, there was only room for goodbye.

"I'm so sorry, Joey," I whispered into the darkness.

The Nubble Lighthouse stood high and tall and brave, and I liked to think that I was being strong and brave too. I didn't want him to leave, not at all. But the damage had been done. I'd made my bed, and I needed to lie in it. It was true that Gerry's drinking had gotten worse, and being his wife wasn't at all what I'd imagined, but I had made a commitment, and I would stay true to that. And now I was making the decision to end things with Joey Chase.

"I'm sorry too," he whispered. He softly kissed my forehead. My knees were weak. "If things were different, I would be with you."

"I know," I cried.

"Right here in front of this lighthouse. This is where I would marry you."

I began to cry harder and once again found myself in Joey Chase's arms. He smelled of cigars and salt air. "I know it's wrong, but I do love you, Joey."

"I love you too, Gwen."

Footsteps on the rocks startled us both, and we turned, stunned to see Gerry standing before us with his arms crossed. His heart-shattering expression included a very serious look in his eyes.

"Gerry! I—"

"Zip it, Dolly," he said, holding up his hand. "I don't want an explanation. I don't need answers. I don't want to know what happened."

"Gerry, I'm leaving town," Joey interrupted. "Elizabeth is all yours. She deserves a father like you, not some nitwit like me."

I backed up and studied the two men. My two men. I truly did love them both. I admired Gerry for his bravery and his courage. I loved Joey for the way he put others before himself, for the way he took care of me, and for the way he needed me back. What was going to happen now? Would they fight each other right at my feet? Or worse? Would Gerry find the words to describe how disgusted he was with me? They couldn't be worse than the words I was using on myself.

"You don't have to leave. I'm leaving."

"Gerry, where are you going?" Suddenly, I didn't know how I should feel. Losing him again to this war…I just didn't think I could do it. Not again.

"I…well…I need to tell you something."

I stepped forward and lost my balance on the rocks. I gripped Joey's wrist for support. If Gerry noticed, he didn't make a fuss.

"Dolly, when I was in France, I met someone."

"Met someone?" I asked, confused.

"A nurse."

"A nurse?"

"Yes, a nurse in my fleet. Her name is Rosemary."

So many questions spun through my mind. The light from the Nubble was suddenly too bright.

"When did you meet her?" Joey asked for me.

He cleared his throat. "Right away. I met her as soon as I was overseas."

"That's why you didn't write," I realized.

"Yes, Dolly," he said. "That's why I didn't write."

I placed my hand over my awestruck face. Hurt, sadness, but also relief rushed through my veins.

Gerry wiped a tear from his eye. "I fell in love with her, Dolly."

I nodded and stared at him, at a loss for words. "You fell in love with your nurse?" I affirmed.

"Yes," he said. "I was going to end it when I found out that you were pregnant, but one of my buddies, who couldn't keep his nose out of my business, helped me do that math, and I knew right away the numbers didn't add up. I knew in my gut the baby wasn't mine."

"I'm so sorry."

"Don't be. Rosemary, my nurse...she saved my life, you know."

"I'm thankful for her then," I whispered.

"Rosemary...that's her name."

My breath caught in my throat. There, standing before me and Joey Chase, was Gerry, a man I was sure I loved. A man I had married. A man who had promised he would come home to me and that we would live a life of happiness. A man I'd cried over day after day and night after night. The same man I had been unfaithful to had also been unfaithful to me.

"I want you two to be together. Joey, I want you to raise your daughter...because I am going to be raising my son." He choked on his words and began to cry.

Joey cried too, and I stared in awe as my two men embraced in a hug that seemed to last forever.

"I didn't mean for this to happen," I cried.

He turned and pulled me close. "Dolly, you have Joey now. I asked him to take care of you, and he sure did a hell of a job of that."

We both laughed a small laugh, and he kissed my forehead like he had done so many times before. "Go on. Be happy, Dolly," he mumbled between sobs. "But listen. My parents just drew up some papers, and that cottage of mine...well, it looks like it's going to be only in the Anderson family now. Which means that you and Mr. Chase here are going to have to find somewhere else to live."

"Okay, Gerry, we will." I winced at the idea of having to leave the Anderson cottage. A piece of me would always be there.

"But listen to me, Dolly. There will always be a special

place for you in my heart." He took my hand and placed it on his chest.

I saw Joey look down at the sand out of the corner of my eye. It was hard to make eye contact with either of them.

"There are some papers that say you can come live at the cottage anytime you want. One hundred dollars for one hundred days. I know it's a lot of money, but the agreement lasts forever."

"One hundred days?" I asked, confused. "That's kind of an odd number, don't you think?"

"That's how many letters you wrote me. And even though things got rough, those letters kept me going."

"Oh, Gerry." I wiped my eyes with my sleeve.

"If you are one hundred years old and change your mind and decide that I'm the man for you, Dolly, you come back, you hear? Or if your daughter Elizabeth ever needs to come back, or her children, or her children's children. One hundred dollars for one hundred days. And if you don't have one hundred dollars, Dolly, I'll take a hundred of these." He bent down and gave me the most passionate kiss we had ever shared.

"Okay, Gerry," I cried.

"And Joey, you better be coming around to the cottage again. I miss my old pal."

"I miss you too, Gerry. I miss you too."

And with that, he turned and walked away, leaving Joey and me in front of the lighthouse by ourselves. We stood hand in hand, watching a man we both loved walk away into his future. It wasn't the happiest of moments, but in the stillness of the night, guided by the Nubble's glowing light, we knew it was going to be okay.

EPILOGUE

NOW- CASSIDY

"So this is beers and sea glass?" Sean laughs, carrying his Solo cup in one hand and mine in the other.

"Yes, it is." I giggle. "Am I boring you?"

"No, you aren't boring me." He laughs. "It's just that I don't see much sea glass."

"It's because the tide is coming in." I laugh. "You have to look harder!"

He kicks up the water around himself and pretends to look. "I don't see any!"

I trudge through the water toward him, spilling my beer in the process. "You aren't trying hard enough," I say again.

The sun is setting behind us on Long Sands Beach, and the landscape is becoming quieter. I feel like I am standing in the middle of a painting. The landscape and the colors of the sky couldn't be more perfect if they tried. As big as the smile on my boyfriend's face glows, it is still no match for mine. Sean places his free hand under my chin and pulls me in for a kiss. I move forward to meet him, but he quickly pulls back. "Wait!" he cries. "I think I see something!"

"Really? It's pretty murky. I don't know how you will..."

I stop short, because Sean Anderson is down on one knee in the ocean, holding up a velvet box—the one from the attic.

"Grandma's ring," I whisper.

"Cassidy Anne Quinn, you are the love of my life. There is nobody I would rather spend the rest of my life with. Nobody but you."

"Sean, are you proposing?"

"Yes!" He laughs. "I'm down on one knee, and I am asking you to marry me!"

"Oh my goodness," I shriek. "Yes! Yes, Sean, I will marry you."

His eyes light up, and I couldn't love him more. "You want to be my wife?" he asks, his tone turning serious.

"Yes! More than anything in this world."

He slides the ring onto my finger and spins me around until we are both dizzy, and we fall into the water. The chill of the sea does not bother either of us one bit.

We climb out of the water, and I lie down on the cold, hard sand. I examine my ring and shriek again with excitement. What a special proposal! What a special man.

He leans over me, his wet shirt stuck tight to his chest, and kisses me again. I don't want this moment to end, and I realize it doesn't have to. This man will be mine forever.

His eyes meet mine, and I pull back, taking in every second of what will soon be a memory, a story that we will tell our kids someday about the day Mommy and Daddy got engaged.

"Cassidy?"

"Yes?"

"Do you promise not to leave me at the altar?"

I punch him in the arm and laugh as he pulls me on top of him, and we kiss once more. "I guess you will have to wait and see."

He laughs, and I kiss him again. "Your words say one thing, but your kiss says another, Cassidy Quinn."

"Oh yeah? What does my kiss say?"

"That you will love me forever."

"Forever and ever," I say. And I do.

ABOUT THE AUTHOR

Stacy Lee is a lifelong resident of New England. She lives in New Hampshire with her incredibly supportive husband, two beautiful children, and two well loved (spoiled) rescue pups. She enjoys spending time in the beautiful and historic town of York Beach, Maine with her family. The Nubble Lighthouse holds a special place in her heart.

Before she started writing women's fiction, Stacy received her bachelor's degree in elementary education with a teacher certification in grades K-8. She taught elementary school and writing courses to students for fourteen years while completing a graduate degree in elementary administration where she graduated with honors. After that, (in an effort to drive her husband completely crazy) decided to switch careers and go to Bible College, where she graduated with a Master's in Christian Ministry with a focus in Homiletics. Finally, when she got tired of taking college courses she decided to do the two things that make her happiest- working for her family business with her best friend and writing. She is thankful for her husband and his ability to bring out the best in her, always.

f 𝕏 ⌾

ALSO BY STACY LEE

Coming Soon!

Be on the lookout for Stacy Lee's next release…

Future Plans

Life's special moments are meant to be celebrated. That's why Hazel Lavigne launched and perfected her own event planning company outside of Fort Lauderdale, Florida. As a single mother in her early thirties, Hazel means business when it comes to her career. But when her daughter's life is suddenly in jeopardy, Hazel has no choice but to pack up and move back to her hometown of York, Maine. Hazel comes to terms with her reality and decides to spend the summer months creating quality memories with her daughter, Ellie. Little does she know that this roller coaster ride she has found herself on is only just beginning. Amidst uncovering relationships both new and old, Hazel will discover that although she is most comfortable in the drivers seat, there are some things we just can't plan.

Made in United States
North Haven, CT
20 August 2023

40530441R00109